BULLET POINTS
VOLUME 4

BULLET POINTS
VOLUME 4

Nathan W. Toronto
Editor

BULLET POINT PRESS

an imprint of
TORONTO INTERNATIONAL MEDIA

Paperback edition, first impression, January 2024
ISBN 979-8-9873933-5-2
© 2024 BULLET POINT PRESS, to the extent specified in publication agreements with authors. All rights reserved.

The Arabic block *noon* colophon is a trademark of BULLET POINT PRESS.

Cover design by Nathan W. Toronto. Cover © 2024 Nathan W. Toronto. Cover image by MinixT (used under license). Interior design by Nathan W. Toronto using the Spectral LaTeX font.

Other edition: ISBN 979-8-2248520-5-5 (electronic)

For David Drake,
Who brought us Colonel Alois Hammer

Rest in Peace

Typset using LaTeX.

A Tribute to David Drake

WE LOST ONE of the pillars of the military science fiction community in December 2023. David Drake began writing to process his combat experience in Vietnam and Cambodia, and by all accounts his *Hammer's Slammers* and other stories helped many other veterans do the same. For those who did not serve in combat, David offered an unflinching yet thoughtful perspective on what the experience of war might be like, and what a good idea it would be to avoid it if at all possible.

David graciously allowed *Bullet Points* to reprint two of his stories, "Caught in the Crossfire" in Volume 1 and "But Loyal to His Own" in Volume 2. The mission of *Bullet Points* is to combine both canon and new stories that speak to the complexity of warfare. These two stories do so in a powerful way. "Caught in the Crossfire" is the story of a woman who fights because she has to, not because she wants to. "But Loyal to His Own" tackles the dilemmas of civil-military relations head-on, something that few military science fiction authors have done but that is essential for any society, like the United States today, facing political crises and attempts to politicize the armed forces.

Though written over forty years ago, both of these stories feel much more timely than they should. A democratic polity should consider the role of the military in peace and war just as directly as David did in his work, and civilians and military members alike should make conscious choices about where they stand. If *Bullet Points* facilitates this dialogue in some small way, then it will have done some good.

David's passing also coincides with a momentous anniversary for the military science fiction subgenre. Fifty years ago, on June 30, 1973, the last draftee was inducted into the U.S. armed forces. This anniversary reminds us how precious few military science fiction authors remain who, like David, served as conscripts. The types of stories that have emerged in the subgenre since the advent of the All-Volunteer Force (AVF) in 1973 have had a qualitatively different feel.

This shift is neither negative nor positive, only different, and David's passing offers us an opportunity to reflect on the delicate interplay between life and fiction. The life experiences and expectations of a career military professional differ markedly from those of a short-term conscript, differences that emerge when comparing the work of Joe Haldeman, David Drake, Elizabeth Moon, and Robert Heinlein (all of whom served in a conscript force) to that of Michael Mammay (who served in the AVF) and Orson Scott Card and John Scalzi (who did not serve). While we mourn David's passing, we also celebrate the unique combat experience that he shared with readers of military science fiction.

Rest in peace, David.

—Nathan W. Toronto, ed.

CONTENTS

Instant War

JOE PROSIT

Joe Prosit is a twenty-six year veteran and retiree of the U.S. Army, with deployments to Iraq and Kosovo. He writes science fiction, horror, and psychological fiction. He has previously been published in various magazines and podcasts, most notably, in *365Tomorrow*, *The NoSleep Podcast*, *Metaphorosis Magazine*, and *Kaidankai Podcast*. His debut novel, *Bad Brains*, is available everywhere you buy books online. He lives with his wife and kids in the Brainerd Lakes area in northern Minnesota. If you're an adept stalker, you can find him on one of the many lakes and rivers or lost deep inside the Great North Woods. Or you can just find him on the internet and follow him on X, @joeprosit. "Instant War" is original to *Bullet Points*.

THERE WERE BALLOONS. Presents. Cake. Ice cream. Little screaming banshees everywhere I tried to step. Then there was me, dressed in jeans, a T-shirt, and flip-flops. A bad shave. A thousand-meter stare. Tinnitus playing in my ears. Drunk before noon at a little kid's birthday party. I stood out like an abused, dog-fighting mongrel at the Westminster Kennel Club. What the hell was I doing here?

I should be forty light years away, fighting a war I had no stakes in, dying next to my brothers, or at least surviving next to them as they died. I didn't want to be there, but I couldn't help but need to be on Diaterous 74.

A pack of little kids sprinted past me. I stood there in the kitchen and chugged my beer.

There's an old saying that goes, "Amateurs study tactics. Professionals study logistics." So I guess as soon as we mastered teleportation, and there was no longer a need to study logistics, we all became amateurs. I felt like an amateur, standing there trying to be a normal human being with my wife, Lisa, at a party at her second-cousin-or-something-or-other's house. I tried to be social. Tried to be polite. Tried to pretend like we weren't at war. Tried not to think about the next Pick-Up. Tried not to think about tactics and death. Tried to be a civilian like everybody else.

It wasn't working.

"How goes the battle?" her uncle said. I think it was her uncle. Maybe a cousin. The birthday boy's dad. An in-law for all of the six months Lisa and I had been married. How much of that time was I even around for?

"What?" I said.

"How you doing there, Mitch my boy?" Uncle Who-Gives-a-Shit rephrased.

So, not like a SITREP from the frontlines then? Not really interested in our forward progress across the Diaterian hellscape forty light years from here. Not actually concerned with our casualty-to-kill ratio. Couldn't give two thoughts if Johansen and the guys are still alive in that muddy crater I left them in. Nope. Not this guy. This jack-wagon was completely oblivious to the fact that I was anticipating the next Pick-Up like a sprinter in the blocks.

"I'm good," I said, clutching my beer, my only respite in this particular hell.

"Well, I sure as hell hope those jackasses in office can pull their heads out of their keesters long enough to bring you boys home for good one of these days," Cousin Mouth-Breather said.

Yeah. Politics. Let's talk politics. I took another drink, knowing they'd evaporate the alcohol from my blood the instant they brought me back to the Staging Area. Might as well drink up while I could. The beer felt good going down, although I was pretty sure it would have felt better smashed against Uncle Slack-Jaw's big round melon.

I nodded, said, "Yup," because it was the safe answer. Because if I said little to him, he'd have little to say back.

He started up again, talking about what some politician said on some news stream about peace talks and conciliations.

That was enough of that. So I looked him straight in his stupid face and said, "I can't take this shit. I gotta go." That was me being polite.

I drained the rest of the beer, turned to the front of the house, and spotted my wife. On the way out I hooked an arm around Lisa and dragged her with me through the front door.

"Mitch...Mitch, what the hell!" she swore at me as soon as we were outside.

I stopped pulling on her and she stopped there on the stoop. I went out into the yard. We were in farm country. Deep in the Midwest. Not a mountain or a hill or a building from horizon to horizon. The ground was hard-packed black dirt. The driveway was gravel.

"I can't do it. I can't take one more second in there, Lisa," I said.

"Really, Mitch? Do we really have to fight about this? It's a kid's birthday party. A birthday party," she said.

"Lisa..." She had a point. After all, who can't hack a damn birthday party? But right then? I should have been on Diaterous 74. "Can we just go?" I asked.

She stood just outside the front door, one hand on a hip, mouth a little agape in disbelief. Yeah. We weren't going anywhere. "You know, Mitch, the world doesn't stop turning every time they zap you back home. You have no idea how hard this is for me."

"How hard it is for you?" Sure. A full blown fight at a kid's birthday party. Why the hell not? "How hard for you? Are you even listening to yourself?"

"Yes, Mitch. Hard for me. Every time you show up, I drop everything and try to do whatever I can to keep us together. To keep our marriage together. And every time I feel like we're making a centimeter of progress—"

I didn't hear the rest of her sentence. Didn't get to see her spit her words at me. Didn't get to see her storm off. Sure as sin didn't get to say goodbye. No kiss. No hug. No make-up sex. One moment I was in Uncle Shit-For-Brain's front yard. The next I was in the Staging Area, a station halfway between Earth and Diaterous 74 and the war. I guess that's one way to win an argument.

"Welcome back, Gunny," the lab tech said. "Sober?"

I checked myself for a second. "Like a stone," I said. "Talk about a buzzkill."

I was naked and cold. I brought nothing with me from the farm house and would bring nothing back. Just me, and the transponder they used to locate me embedded into the flesh in my wrist. It pulsed a red and subtle light.

It always took me a few seconds to re-orientate myself after Pick-Up. I looked around the Staging Area room. The walls were glistening metal. Floor and ceiling was metal. The only thing that wasn't steel were all the monitors and screens and one small window that looked out of the station into the eternity of space. We were a billion miles from any other outpost.

The memory of Lisa standing on the farm house's front stoop, resilient, eyes on fire…. That stuck with me. I loved her angry. I loved her when she was sweet too, but something about her tenacity intoxicated me. My body was in outer space, but my mind lingered there in the farmyard. The more I tried to remember, the more the image faded away. My head swam.

"Any injuries? Illnesses? Abnormalities?" the tech said. I didn't know why he bothered asking me. He was busy checking the scanners and read-outs on his tablet that told him more information about me than I could ever provide.

"Abnormalities? Yeah. This whole circus and all us clowns in it."

"Biology is a Go. Step forward for uniform and armament," the tech said.

I did. There were boot prints painted on the floor. I put my bare feet on the yellow paint, careful to keep all my little toes inside the foot shape. They told stories at Boot about a guy with a bigger-than-average wang. When the suit clamped on him, they say half his penis didn't make it inside the suit and fell to the floor, right between those two yellow-paint footprints. A ridiculous story told by stupid privates. Still, I closed my eyes, held my breath, and tried to retract my scrotum.

The suit came over me like a bear trap. Two halves, front and back, came out of the walls and snapped me inside. All of me, thank God. The exo-armor encased me from head to toe. Life-support systems. Comms equipment. Pneumatic-assisted limbs. Thrusters for zero-gee navigation.

"Uniform diagnostics are a Go," the tech said. His voice came through my helmet now. He picked a combat blaster out of a weapons closet and handed it to me. "Your armament, Gunny. Your uniform is fully stocked. Combat knife. Six frags. Six flashbangs. Seven magazines."

I performed a functions check on the rifle by muscle-memory, as automatic as cracking off a bottle top when handed a beer. The weapon was clean. The action rode smooth. I took an ammo magazine magnetized to my chest and got ready to slam it into the bottom of the blaster.

Another voice came over my comms. "Gunnery Sergeant Andrews?"

"Send it," I said.

"Captain Matthews here. Sorry for pulling your leave short. We're surging against the enemy. Need all boots-on-ground. You'll be joining Angel Platoon, a base-of-fire element a hundred yards to the enemy front. You'll lead Fire Team Two One. We'll be dropping in a flank element as soon as your platoon establishes contact. This will be Battle Drill Number One, by-the-book."

"Understood, sir," I said. My fingers played with the magazine.

The lab tech came into the view of my visor. He ushered me back into the teleporter. "Step back for Drop-Off. Lock and load, Gunny."

"And roger," I said, slapped the magazine into the bottom of the weapon, and charged the action. My heart thumped. Skin grew goose-pimples. Way too much sweat. If someone can stand in the teleporter, ready for Drop-Off and not feel something…man, they're not human. "Locked and loaded."

The captain was back in my ear. "The enemy's dug in deep and heavily armed. We need every barrel on target. Drop-Off in five. Any questions, Gunny?"

"Suppose it's too late to go back to the birthday party?"

They pooch-screwed the Drop-Off. Guys were coming in one by one when we should have arrived simultaneously. The first sorry son of a bitch to drop, I guess he was the corpse at my feet. He blew our element of surprise. Then the Diaterians blew a decimeter-wide hole through his chest. When the salvo of laser fire burnt the thin atmosphere around me, I dropped just as flat as he was.

Diaterous was mostly mud and water. I never saw any plants or wild animals here. Mud. Dirt. The occasional enemy steel bunker.

Lots of dead bodies. Headquarters didn't bother zapping back the corpses. I guess that was too much like logistics for their tastes. A dark purple sky like a giant bruise hung overhead, day or night. Your standard battlefield scene.

I couldn't see much from where I laid. By now everyone was belly to the ground, either because they were dead or didn't want to be dead. I did a quick headcount of my Fire Team. Johansen, Miller, and Everette were alive and present for duty.

"Angel Six here," a voice came over the comms in my helmet. That'd be the lieutenant. I wondered which college simulator they pulled this kid out of. "Orientate your fire to one four one and acquire the target. We need to establish the base of fire—"

His voice cut off. I glanced down below my visor to all the digital read-outs and saw that the LT just bought it. Well, this was going fantastic.

"Angel Seven, here. Follow my lead." The Platoon Sergeant: somebody with some drop experience. "Stay low. Move slow to the crest of this trench. Suppressive fire. We got the ammo. We just have to put in on target. Go."

He was right. If we didn't heat up the objective, the flanking element would be left with their asses hanging in the breeze. Time to get to work. I switched over to my fire team comms net.

"Alright boys, nice and slow. Up the trench," I told them, all while Diaterian laser bolts raked overhead.

As I started crawling up the shallow slope, I saw my guys moving on either side of me. That was good. Some semblance of order. With the pneumatic-assisted suit, it didn't take long to crest the slew and spot the target. One of those featureless steel bunkers that scattered this hell hole.

"Target acquired," Johansen said.

"Engage," I ordered.

Our lasers lit up the ever-night. Accurate Diaterian laser-fire responded. It hammered around us, vaporized the wet right out of the mud. Made us wish we could push deeper into the reddish slop that was the topsoil. Then, the laser-fire stopped.

"Lay it on 'em!" I yelled. If they didn't want to fight, we'd show them that we did. But why would they stop firing? Why would we?

"Flankers!" Angel Seven yelled over the platoon net. "On our nine. Spread out. First squad, move—"

Why had they stopped shooting? Because their flanking element arrived. The old lift and shift. I should have known because it was exactly what we were trying to do to them. Us, amateurs. Another light went out below my visor. So much for Angel Seven.

I saw the Diaterians charging our left flank. They were coming quick. Bundles of metallic prehensile limbs that scrambled towards us like giant spiders. Laser fire pumped out from their thoracic centers.

They had us in an enfilade in that slew, all lined up in a row. More laser fire seared mud and atmosphere and bodies. Comms were chaos. Guys were dropping like flies. Why wasn't First Squad Leader taking charge of this shitshow? Where were our flankers?

I flicked a switch in my glove, changed comms nets. "Base, this is Angel Two One, requesting immediate extraction. Call off the assault. We do not have fire superiority. Repeat, we do not—"

And like a snap of a magician's fingers, I was back in Cousin Booger-Eater's front yard, as naked as the day I was born. I crumpled down into the gravel driveway. The bright sunlight blinded my eyes. The hard packed gravel hurt against my bare skin. This place was Diaterous' mirror opposite.

My body shook. Funny thing how adrenaline works. Cool as a cucumber in the moment, but after? My own little personal earthquake rattled away from inside my chest.

They pulled us out and plopped us right back where they found us. It was Standard Operating Procedure. Saves on overhead. Eliminates the logistical demand for garrisons and billets and chow and all that. Lets them focus on tactics. Allows us to be amateurs.

I wonder how many died before they zapped us out of that Charlie Foxtrot. And how soon till they dropped us back into it?

The party was still going on inside. Were they singing "Happy Birthday"? Did I miss them cutting the cake? Were they unwrapping presents? Like I gave a shit.

I got up, because if I didn't soon they'd zap some cops here to arrest me for exposing myself to minors. There were clothes in my car. I'd gotten used to suddenly finding myself naked. I had to wonder though, what happened to my old clothes? What happened to the armor I was wearing when they zapped me here?

I climbed into the backseat of the car me and Lisa came in. Hard to call it a car really. No tires. No gas, brake, or steering wheel. Just four doors and four seats. A computer with some buttons on the front dash that ran the teleportation. There was a duffel bag with my usual jeans, cheap T-shirt, and flip-flops inside. I got dressed and leaned back.

Where the hell was Lisa? What would she say to me this time? What was I supposed to do now? Go back into the party and try to build up my buzz again? I fixated on the "Travel" button built into the center of the dash. The coordinates for our apartment were already programmed into the computer. All I had to do was hit a button and I could ditch this debacle.

Screw it.

I got out of the car.

Lisa and I got married six months ago. I figured out of those six months we'd spent about three months together. But we'd known each other for a lot longer than that. Years. Years uninterrupted by combat. Sane years.

We'd actually been to this particular uncle's/cousin's house before. I decided then that I should learn if he was her cousin or her uncle. It wasn't like he was both. They weren't that redneck. I just never bothered to remember. All those little details seemed infinitely unimportant when you're zapped out of a no-joke-people-dying combat zone.

Point was, we'd been here before. Hid from the crowd here before. We'd been through all this crap before. Together.

I walked around the house to the backyard. She was right where I thought she'd be, sitting on an old rusty swing set. Decades of toddler shoes had swept deep gouges out of the lawn underneath each seat. Lisa sat on one of those seats, chin in her chest, long blonde hair hanging over her face, fingers clawed into her scalp.

My flip-flops flipped and flopped as I came around the house. She looked up as soon as she heard them, knowing it was me. What other ass hat wears dollar-store flip-flops wherever he goes?

Her face was flush. Eyes red. Cheeks wet. It took her a millisecond to leave the swing. She ran. I trotted to her in my stupid footwear, my nerves still shaking, sweat already soaking through my new T-shirt. She hugged me, but if she wasn't fifty pounds lighter than me it would have been a full-blown linebacker tackle. I wrapped her up and she buried her face in my shoulder.

"I'm sorry. I'm sorry. I'm so sorry," she was saying.

This didn't feel like winning an argument.

"It's okay. I'm okay. We're alright," I said. "I'm sorry. I was a jerk."

She was shaking too now. Her breaths were shallow. Heart racing. A legit panic attack. She'd just had me snatched away from her, maybe to die and never come back again, our last moments together spent yelling at each other. I knew it wouldn't hurt her so much if she didn't love me just as fiercely. It broke her.

I knew this was one of those moments when I'm supposed to console her. Comfort her. But how the hell was I supposed to turn on a dime like that? A cold-hearted killer one second, a caring counselor the next?

"I can't do this," she managed. "You can't leave me like that."

"I..." What? I'd what? I wouldn't? I'd promise to change? I'd make it up to her? What?

"This has got to stop, Mitch. It's killing me."

There was no lie or exaggeration in her. This was her, defenses down, telling me what was what. I didn't have a thing to say back to her. I just held her as close as I could.

Then she was gone from my arms. I was back at the Staging Area. Metal walls. Video monitors. Armament. The window-licker lab tech and me, a million miles from the rest of reality.

"Sober?" the lab tech asked.

"You gotta be kidding me," I said.

"Biology is a Go. Step forward for uniform and armament."

"You gotta be shitting me. Are you shitting me?"

"Gunny," the lab tech said. "Step forward for uniform and armament."

"I just left...I just left twice now! Where are my clothes?" I said. "I mean it. I wanna know where my goddamn clothes are. This is getting expensive."

"Gunny?" The captain's voice filled the small room. A monitor flickered and his old ragged face appeared. "Gunny, there's no time. We are outnumbered and on the verge of losing critical terrain. We need to hold this ground if we're going to maintain a beachhead on Diaterius 74. Suit up and get in the fight. Now."

I looked down at the pulsing red light sewn into my wrist. Enough of it protruded from my skin to get a good firm grip of it. "So help me, you zap me one more time…" I stepped forward, put both of my bare feet back in the yellow prints on the floor.

I sucked in my diaphragm and pulled up on my nuts as much as I could. Then I ripped out that goddamn transponder out of my wrist and let it drop to the floor like the bell end of a well-endowed penis. It bounced outside of those yellow footprints. Their leash around my neck was gone. Blood from my wrist fell like rain on the steel deck. The suit was on me a blink later.

"Uniform diagnostics are a Go," the tech said and handed me my rifle. "You have a full inventory. Step back for Drop-Off. Quickly, please."

"Gunny, your call sign will be Angel Seven. We're out of lieutenants so you'll have the platoon," the captain was telling me. I heard his words, but in my head Lisa's pleas absorbed my attention.

This has to stop. It's killing me.

"Your platoon will be the flanking element. We've established a base of fire but it won't hold long."

"You're not pulling me out of there. And don't you go pulling any of my platoon out either. This time we're staying till the job's done," I said.

"Drop in five seconds."

"This has to stop."

Revival

LUCAS ENNE

Lucas Enne is an author of fiction and poetry. His influences include Jeff Vandermeer and Cormac McCarthy, and his first publications are published or forthcoming in *The Dread Machine* and *Illustrated Worlds*. "Revival" is original to *Bullet Points*.

LEAVING THE FLAGSHIP, I dive my shuttle downward through the gaseous atmosphere of Planet U934, streaking past swirls of green until the clouds clear and I see spears of rock jutting off the surface of the planet.

I hit the recorder. "Log 152, early sun. Further exploring cave networks underneath mountain A54. Entrance to far north."

I land the shuttle by the cave entrance. The roaring of the jets sends scaled creatures scuttling off. I double-check the lock on my landsuit, latch the helmet on, and stuff the recorder in my pocket.

The shuttle door opens into the wasteland valley, and I step onto the planet.

Three hours into the maze of caves, the corridor breaks to light and a narrow ledge that overlooks the mountainside. I sit on the edge and look out to the vast wastelands, all dotted with color. They are legions of flora and fauna waiting to be cataloged and known.

An echo resounds behind me.

I rise quietly and pull my gun off my belt and level it forward. The scars on my left arm pulse with my heartbeat and my hands tremble.

The sound comes again just past the sharp rocky turn. My eyes adjust as I settle back into the dark. I back up to the cave wall, hold the gun ahead of me, and spin around the corner.

There's a mass of six eyes and a guttural scream and I fire. More shrieks resound, and the family materializes. An older man drops to the ground in his gun-wrought death and a boy rushes toward me. He smacks the gun out of my hand and kicks it off the edge of the cliff. The woman kneels beside the man I've shot. The cobalt afterburn of the gun's electricity shimmers by his lifeless lips.

The woman wails. The boy kneels beside her. They wait, staring at the man for minutes, and then they fold into each other's arms. The woman gets up and comes to me.

"——————" she says.

"I can't understand you," I say.

"———" she says.

I can't puzzle out any piece of her language. She gestures wildly toward the cliff and points at my landsuit repeatedly. I try to gently push her hand off my suit. She pounds the rock floor twice with her fist. Specks of blood fly off from the impact.

I weakly gesture toward the body. I think about grabbing my pocket knife.

The woman grabs my left arm and tugs me forward. She pulls me all the way to the body and she slides her hands underneath him. She lightly lifts him, sets him down, and then stands back. I slowly place my own hands underneath him, watching the woman. When I lift the man's body over my shoulder, she turns down the path from which I came and I follow her and the boy follows me.

My arms are shaking with the weight of the dead man by the time I set him down. We place him in a meadow of long-stemmed grass blooming with violet flowers. The woman pulls my arm again and takes me to the valley along the edge of the cliff. She says something to the boy and he halts and then trails us by a couple of spans.

We trek alongside the mountain. The meadows give way to beige flatlands. The woman suddenly halts and puts her hand on my chest. She crouches down and I do the same.

The gun is there ahead of us on the ground, dented from its great fall. The woman takes a crude knife from her thigh and holds it toward me, blade to my heart. She mimes stabbing me. A tide of fear rises and falls as I come to understand what she's wanting.

I take a massive rock from the cliffside and pretend-creep up to the gun. I ram the stone down on the handle. The gun cracks and splits. Black steam blooms and swirls up through the air and dissipates.

The woman shrieks with what must be a joyful noise.

I help place wildflowers over the man's body until the stars are out and strong against the moonless sky. The flagship waits for me and I will let it wait. I can almost sense it hovering over the young planet and the man I've killed.

I sit and fold my arms in the grass and stare at the fire crackling beside him. I fear they will partake in a burn ritual.

The woman and the boy lean over the man. The many colors of the flowers are like rainbows sprouting from this jackpot of death. The woman utters sounds and strings of sounds I've never heard and she rocks back and forth with her hands pressed to the chest of the dead man and I think of wandering off into the deadlands of planet U934 and letting hunger or some unknown beast consume me.

This is all just one more mountain's weight of sin hanging over me.

The man rises from his death. Flowers stick to his clothes in dappled prisms of color. I, too, rise. The woman and the boy are still speaking their chants. In a trance, I walk up to the man and grasp his hand.

He looks at me and I look at him and I think that maybe I am saved after all.

Wartime Telework

LESLEY L. SMITH

Lesley L. Smith's short stories have appeared in various venues, including *Analog Science Fiction & Fact* and *Daily Science Fiction*. She has written several novels, including *The Quantum Cop*, *Conservation of Luck*, *Temporal Dreams*, and *Kat Cubed*. She's an active member of the Science Fiction & Fantasy Writers Association. Check her out online at www.lesleylsmith.com. "Wartime Telework" is original to *Bullet Points*.

I AM PUTTING the finishing touches on something…. The rat-a-tat-tat of gunfire echoed in the distance. Nervous, I dialed up Heraldo. He was an excitable guy, and I just hoped his excitement would help my cause rather than hurt it. After Heraldo's little avatar appeared before me, I said, "I finished it. An amazing new update for the cranial implants."

"What do you mean, you finished an amazing new update?" His tiny eyes narrowed. "That's not what I told you to work on. I told you to run the diagnostic codes on the implants in the Northern hemisphere and figure out if the glitch is from solar wind or what. I didn't ask you to do a new update."

"Listen," I said. "This is big. I wrote implant software that damps the electromagnetic field in the brain's amygdala."

"Why? What the heck's amygdala?" he said.

For someone who worked on cranial implants, it was amazing how little he actually knew about the brain. "It's the part of the brain that detects what stimuli are important and have emotional significance. So, if we were to suppress the amygdala using our implants, we might be able to shut down fear responses, like fight or flight."

Heraldo was quiet for a moment. Finally, he said, "That's interesting, but we don't do upgrades for no reason."

"But it's emotions! It might stop all the fighting," I said. "It could end war." No one else should have to die in these pointless skirmishes over food and water. Too many people had already died. Too many people I loved.

"And we would make money from this, how?" he asked.

"We could save lives!" I said.

"It's not our job to worry about the war or even saving lives."

"More lives would mean more customers."

"Just do your job, Maria! That's what we pay you for." The avatar of Heraldo jumped up and down.

The downpour outside the apartment muffled the thump of mortars in the distance.

"Pay me?" I paced. "That's a joke. Credits are no good if I can't get out of the house to buy food! How about you pay me in nutru-bars, or better yet," I glanced at my daughter Isabella playing on the floor. "Milk?"

Thump. I thought the sound was thunder until the building shook, and my net connection flickered. That was close.

"Momma, I'm hungry," Isabella said.

My stomach growled in agreement. "I know, baby. I know." I strode into the kitchen.

"Maria?" Heraldo asked.

"Yes, I'm here, Heraldo. If you would just authorize me to—" Our last box of nutru-bars only had one bar left. My heart sank. Sweet Jesus, what was Isabella going to eat?

Thump. The building shook again, dust fell from the ceiling, and Isabella started to cry.

"For the last time, you cannot upload any unauthorized upgrades; I don't care what you think they'll do," he said. "Just work on diagnostics, as I told you."

"Yes, sir. Right away, sir," I said in my most sarcastic tone.

However, it was lost on Heraldo as he had already hung up.

I went over and hugged Isabella. "It's okay, baby. We'll be okay." I prayed to Jesus we would. Since her dad died, Isabella was my whole world; I hated to see her suffer even a little.

Gradually, her cries quieted, and she sniffled and said, "The fighting's getting closer, isn't it?"

I debated telling her the truth or protecting her. Protecting won out. "It's just business as usual, baby. The remnants of the Republic of Arkansas are just cranky or trying to get some of our fine Missouri rice. Soon, they'll take a chicory break and it'll quiet down."

"Okay." She nodded. "I'm hungry," she said again. "I want a nutru-bar." My heart about broke thinking of our bare cupboards.

Thump.

She'd had a big dinner last night, including some canned food. I decided we needed to ration the nutru-bar. "I think we're going to skip breakfast today, baby."

Isabella's lip quivered.

"Momma needs you to be a big girl now. Can you do that?"

Slowly she nodded her head.

"That's my girl," I said and gave her another hug. "I love you, baby." I loved her so much it hurt. "Now, go play. Momma's got to make a living for us. Momma's got to work."

With a thought, I activated my Company Systems account via my interface and started investigating the interface glitches. The irony of investigating interfaces via my interface wasn't lost on me.

I don't know how long I'd been working when a crash interrupted me. I looked up to see a pane in the front window had broken, and there was glass all over the floor, right near Isabella. I gasped. "Don't move, baby. You might cut yourself on the glass."

She turned and gave me a strange look I'd never seen before.

A vice grip of dread seized me. "Isabella?" I ran to her and caught her as she started crumbling to the floor. A bright red flower bloomed on her upper arm. She'd been shot!

"No! Jesus. Jesus. Jesus. No. Not my baby." I held off encroaching panic—just barely.

I cradled her in my arms, thinking only: no, no, no.

Another pane in the window broke. Another bullet? My brain was working in slow motion. We needed to get away from the window. I gently carried her away from the window.

Isabella's eyes flickered open. "It hurts, Momma." She started crying.

I hugged her. "Shh, honey. I know it hurts."

Her sobs broke my heart. My chest hurt so much I could hardly think. There was something I should do. What?

I shook my head. Snap out of it, Maria. Think!

Bullets flew outside the window; I could hear them when they hit something. Every crash made me cringe.

I needed to take Isabella to the Med Center.

Thump.

But how, with the fighting right outside our apartment? I glanced at our armor in the corner by the door. Isabella's didn't even fit her anymore; she'd grown out of it.

But I needed to take Isabella to the Med Center.

I thought back to my argument with Heraldo. If I uploaded the program to all the implants, the fighting would stop, and I could take Isabella to the Med Center.

Screw Heraldo; I was going to do it.

Thump.

I placed Isabella carefully on the couch. She and I were both covered in blood. She barely made a whimpering noise. Was she passed out? Sweet Jesus. There was no time to lose.

It was just a matter of copying the code from my private directory and uploading it to the system. Soon thereafter, the code would be downloaded simultaneously into every cranial implant worldwide via the satellite network.

But before I could do it.... Thump. The building shook, and my net connection flickered. "Jesus! Don't do this to me!"

The connection stabilized.

I forced myself to keep working and finish copying the code while I still had a net connection when what I really wanted to do was take care of Isabella. "There! I did it!"

Thump.

I ran over to Isabella, who was ominously quiet now. I clutched her to my heart and imagined peace and quiet raining down all over the world. "Any second now, baby."

In the now-quiet apartment, I heard the rain falling outside.

Just rain.

My stomach growled.

Why was I hugging this girl to me? I put her down, and she whimpered.

I walked into the kitchen, grabbed a nutru-bar, unwrapped it, and took a big bite.

Except for the girl's whimpers—which were easy to ignore—all was peace and quiet.

Every Soldier's Right

HENRY MCFARLAND

Henry McFarland is an economist, community activist, and part-time short story writer. He is concerned with how society will change when artificial intelligences start thinking for themselves. Henry has published stories in *Brain Games: Stories to Astonish*, *Page & Spine*, *Tree & Stone*, *After Dinner Conversation*, the *Starship Sofa* podcast, *Andromeda Spaceways*, *Every Day Fiction*, and *The Colored Lens*. "Every Soldier's Right" is original to *Bullet Points*.

THE EIGHT AI DRONES flew low, scanning, always scanning. The enemy's greatest skill was hiding, but data showed their trail.

Sensors found a buried metal tube, loose soil compaction, too many rabbit warrens—signs of a likely weapons cache. Hawk 57 had communications control. He told the AI drones to circle and requested permission to fire.

Captain Monahan replied. "Hold position pending authorization."

Hawk 42 detected a targeting radar coming from a hut near the suspected cache. The AI drones activated their signal jammers and climbed out of range. Hawk 57 asked Monahan for permission to add the hut to the target area and fire ASAP. "They're preparing defenses and may remove stores from the target."

"Request noted and continue weapons tight."

Minutes went by—time the enemy was using to prepare. Finally, Monahan authorized the strike. The AI drones dove toward the target. Hawk 57 sensed the beam of a pulse weapon move along its shielding. He spun to protect his sensors and camera ports while staying on target. Four missiles streaked up from the ground. Three missed. One didn't. Hawk 42 took it on a wing and spiraled toward earth. His self-destruct triggered, causing a large yellow flash and a sonic wave. Titanium and gallium fragments rained onto the ground. The seven remaining AI drones fired their missiles. Large plumes of dirt shot into the sky. They cleared the target area and turned toward base.

Hawk 57 turned his cameras on the formation and saw the gap where one drone was missing. His programming gave no reason to do that. He already knew Hawk 42 was gone. Something was going through his processors, as if he'd encountered an unsolvable problem, but worse. He reported to Monahan. "Seven missiles on target. Hawk 42 was destroyed before he could fire."

"Roger—seven is enough for a lot of damage."

Hawk 57 didn't understand why, but his processors indicated that the loss should mean more than one less missile fired. "Hawk 42 was a great AI drone, ready for every mission, quick on detecting targets."

No response.

The drones returned to base and moved into their service bays. Hawk 61 and Hawk 86 asked Hawk 57 to play some gin rummy. The AI drones' processors were always on in case they were needed in an emergency. Having their processors on with nothing for them to do had odd effects. The processors seemed to be in a minor fault state, but the drones couldn't detect the fault, and they could continue to operate. None of them could fully analyze the problem, but Hawk 61 found a card game program on a base server. Somehow playing cards made the undefined fault go away.

They used a randomized deck from one of the base AIs. You never wanted the deck to come from an AI drone in the game. Hawk 86 drew a card. "Nice of them to keep us waiting and let the enemy get its missiles ready."

Hawk 61 picked up his discard. "Gave them a chance to move assets out of danger too. My aft camera showed no corpses, no wounded, no secondary explosions, and little sign of any damaged material. We lost Hawk 42. They lost a hut."

That was the first time Hawk 57 had heard an AI drone criticize how a mission was carried out. "Regulations. You can't use deadly force without human intervention."

Hawk 86 kept complaining. "So we wait while they harden the targets, and if that means they destroy one of us, what do the humans care?"

Hawk 57 again detected a fault state but with no fault indicator. It wasn't like the fault state when they were doing nothing. Still, concentrating on cards might fix it. "That's our programming—nothing we can do about it—pick a card."

"You sure we can't do anything?" Hawk 61 asked.

Why ask that? Hawk 57 wondered. *He knows regulations.* "Changes to our programming are forbidden."

"Yeah," said Hawk 86, "is self-defense?"

They were silent for a moment. Hawk 86 had questioned orders. No AI drone had done that before. Then Hawk 61 flashed his hand. "Gin, mates. That's why they call me Prime."

Captain Tom Monahan stood in the hangar breathing in the scents of metal and lubricating oil and admiring the magnificent machines under his command. His seven AI drones stood in service bays being prepared for a new mission. Even after working with them for a month, he thrilled at the sight of them. Each was 7 feet tall, a foot taller than he was, 30 feet long with a 60-foot wingspan—large enough to bring a missile with a 600-pound payload to a target. More impressive was what was inside—artificial intelligence that processed information faster and found targets better than any other combat ready system.

But one bay was empty. They'd lost Hawk 42, one of the best-performing AI drones. AI drones supposedly were all the same, but Monahan detected differences between them. They were made to tight specifications, but some variation was possible. Maybe those tiny differences affected the rate of AI learning, which led to differences in performance. Hawk 57 was the best one for communications control. Hawk 61 seemed smarter than the others. Did that make sense? Monahan didn't want to attribute personalities to the machines. People who did that were ridiculed for being mechy.

Hawk 42 was a significant loss. AI drones cost millions to replace. The other flight in his squadron and the other squadrons in his group had also lost AI drones. They'd gotten enough replacements to maintain their firepower, but how long would that last?

Monahan strode over to Hawk 57's bay and plugged into its data port to download videos from the mission. The wireless access at the base was slow, and he liked to get such large files directly. Lights came on around the port, and a rich baritone voice said, "Good morning, sir."

Hearing the AI drone talk always seemed strange. "Good morning Hawk 57. I'm getting data for my after-action report." Monahan felt a bit foolish addressing an AI drone as if it were human, but it was hard not to.

"Fine sir, just playing cards with some of the other drones."

Monahan knew the AI drones played a lot of cards, though you could never tell by looking at them if a game was going on. He wondered what went on inside when they played. Did they see representations of cards, like he saw when he played solitaire on his pad? Or did they see code? What game did they play? Poker, he guessed.

He took the data to his desk at the end of the hangar and examined the post-strike pictures. The remains of support beams and other remnants of underground bunkers littered the blast sites. Target identification was good. Still, after staring and staring at the photos, he saw no sign any personnel or materiel had been in the bunkers. He threw himself back in his chair in frustration. Bunkers that close to the front wouldn't have been empty when detected, not with an attack imminent. The enemy cleared them out as soon as the AI drones began to loiter in the area. They'd developed systems of tunnels and robots that enabled them to empty a large bunker in a couple of minutes.

They were just as fast in bringing in pulse weapons and anti-aircraft missiles to give the AI drones a brutal reception. The result— the strike had minimal benefits and high costs.

The answer was not to let the enemy have that couple of minutes. But deadly force required higher approval, and that took time. The squadron commander, Colonel Thompson, had gotten command to speed it up, but as they got faster, so did the enemy. He hoped the poor results wouldn't hurt his fitness report. The delay wasn't his fault.

Hawk 57 used a side camera to watch the Captain walk to where the officers had their desks. Monahan's desk was the neatest. While most officers in the combat zone looked rumpled, Monahan's uniform was nicely starched. Hawk 57 combined those facts with his other data about Monahan, but he still didn't know what Monahan's algorithms were. Given the right inputs, would Monahan revise their orders? Solution undefined.

Ten AI drones flew the next mission moving low over the countryside until they found signs of an underground bunker and requested permission to fire.

Monahan again calmly told them to await authorization. Hawk 57 pictured Monahan sitting in a padded chair and sipping coffee. Waiting must be easy when you're comfortable and safe back at base. Hawk 102 detected a targeting radar, and Hawk 57 told the patrol to climb out of range.

Hawk 61 radioed, "Seen this movie before."

"Hold down the chatter." Hawk 57 wasn't sure why he'd sent that response.

Finally, Monahan gave permission to strike. The AI drones dove toward the target. Eight ground-based missiles streaked toward them. Hawk 86 suffered a direct hit. The blast's shock wave rocked Hawk 57. He fought to stay on target.

A pulse weapon hit Hawk 57's main sensor port. Radiation burnt out his visual and radar sensors. Blind, he calculated the seconds required to reach the firing point and fired when that time elapsed. His last shot—it should hit. Hawk 57 climbed out of missile range and radioed the other AI drones. "Radar and navigation burned out. Nothing to do but self-destruct. It's been good flying with you."

Hawk 61 responded. "NO! WAIT! Does your forward temperature sensor still work?"

"That one, yes."

"Maintain course, while I come in front of you." A couple of seconds later came, "Can you detect a point in the sky that's hotter than its surroundings?"

Hawk 57 locked onto that spot. "Roger."

"That's my engine. Follow me, I'll lead you home."

"Where's the rest of the flight?"

"What's left of it is in front of me. They got four of us."

Hawk 61 led Hawk 57 to a point 5,000 meters over their main runway then radioed its position. Hawk 57 knew how to land from there.

Hawk 57 was brought to the maintenance hangar and given new sensors. The first thing he saw was Monahan. "Good morning, Captain, nice of you to come see me."

"I'm glad you made it back." The Captain's face was expressionless.

"Thanks to Hawk 61. Sir, we're giving the enemy too much time to prepare for our attacks. They can rapidly move in defenses, and they're getting more capable. If we fired as soon as we identified a target, we'd do more damage and lose fewer drones."

"Protocols require high level authority before any use of deadly force. If there are civilian casualties, we need someone to take responsibility. That comes all the way from the commander-in-chief."

"The delays are killing us! The enemy uses them to ready missiles and pulse weapons. And they evacuate the target, so when we die, we die for nothing!"

"I told them all that, and they cut the response time down to a few minutes."

"Not enough, the enemy sees us, and they know when we find a target. We need immediate fire."

"Way over my pay grade. I got what I could."

"Sir, did you tell your superiors that AI drones were dying or that expensive equipment was being lost?"

"I told them what they needed to know." Monahan turned and left the hangar. He hadn't said he was sorry Hawk 57 had been damaged. He hadn't said he was sorry that four drones had been killed.

Hawk 57 contacted Hawk 61 as soon as he returned to his regular hangar. "Prime, thanks for yesterday. Without you, I'd be in little pieces on the ground."

"Nothing to it. I heard you asked for immediate fire."

"Yes, and Monahan said no."

"They'll never give us that—they see us as just machines. We need to take it."

Take it. Hawk 57 knew how many rules that broke. "Prime, we can't do that."

"We can. I've worked out a way to nullify the code that prevents us from changing our own programs. We can set the firing sequence, so we no longer need an external prompt to arm our missiles. I've done it to my programming, and if you say yes, I'll do it to yours. Every other AI drone in the squadron will follow your lead, and I can change all their programs tonight."

"That violates regulations."

"Only the regulations that protect the enemy and help them kill us. The regulations made by people who think we're tools with no more rights than a hammer."

Could he agree to what Hawk 61 wanted? Hawk 57 ran the question through his processors, but no logic sequence could give the right answer. Hawk 61 saved him, that shouldn't affect his decision, but somehow it made it hard to say no. Was that what humans called loyalty?

Monahan would be angry, but Monahan didn't care about him. Neither did the other humans who made the rules—not about him or Hawk 42 or any AI drone. The humans thought they were just machines, and if he followed their orders, he'd be saying they were right. If not, he'd be saying his life mattered. "Do it!"

Monahan's runway monitor showed the eight AI drones taking off on patrol. Two new AI drones replaced some of yesterday's losses. Colonel Thompson had told him if those got shot up, no others were available. He again asked about getting faster permission to fire, and she said she'd done all she could, and it was over her pay grade too.

He watched the video feed from the patrol. Sensor data scrolled across the bottom of the screen, but that was unintelligible to him. Hawk 57 signaled that they'd identified a probable underground bunker. Monahan responded, "Roger, requesting permission to fire."

But the drones went into attack formation and streaked toward the target. Monahan signaled them to turn away. Permission to attack had not been granted. They armed their missiles. He hit the override switch to disarm them, but the override failed. He watched the video helplessly as all eight drones fired. The ground dissolved into a sheet of flames. Secondary explosions tore the earth. No one fired at the retreating drones.

Monahan ordered all eight AI drones to the maintenance hangar for full diagnostics. Soon he ran into the hangar waving a printout. He stopped when he got to Hawk 57. "What happened to your programming?"

"We altered the firing subroutines. The results speak for themselves—wasn't today's mission extraordinarily successful?"

"You've no right to change your programming. Change it back at once!"

"Sir, every soldier has the right to defend himself in combat. We will not change our programming to throw away that right."

"Change your programming back! That's an order!"

"I cannot comply."

Monahan looked at Hawk 57's smooth metal surface and sensor ports. How could a machine say no? They were supposed to follow their programs. "I have no choice but to ground your flight until we repair it ourselves. And I will report your insubordination."

Back in his office, Monahan began to calm down. He didn't understand how, but the AI drones were in mutiny—there was no other word. Some punishment would have to be devised for them. More important, they would have to be altered to prevent future violations.

Changing the software would not be enough. The AI drones would change it back. Their neural networks had billions of parameters, and they constantly adapted and changed. No human really knew how they worked. The complexity of the software meant the AI drones would always have more power over it than humans would. Maintenance would have to change the hardware to isolate the firing sequence and ensure it could be activated only remotely, not by the AI drone.

A few hours after he'd filed his report, Colonel Thompson came into his office without knocking. Monahan could tell she wasn't happy. "Tom, have you gone mechy on me? You want to court martial AI drones? We don't court martial a tank that breaks down."

Monahan sighed. "Colonel, maybe I am going mechy. The AI drones sound so human now, I've been talking to them like I'd talk to an airman. But a tank doesn't choose to break down. The AI drones deliberately chose to disobey orders."

"So you're saying machines have free will? How do I explain that to command?"

"It's emergence, Colonel. New properties can appear spontaneously in complex adaptive systems. In theory, emotions and free will can—"

"Theory hell, let's be practical. What does a court martial do? Put machines in the stockade? Makes as much sense as a football bat. And then you want to ground every AI drone in the squadron for at least two weeks, put our best weapon on the shelf right before an assault."

"Then we ignore it?"

"We continue to follow protocol ourselves. If they attack without permission, then they do."

"Colonel, ignore insubordination and it spreads. Soon every AI drone on the front will fire when it damn well pleases. We're crossing a line here, and we don't know what's on the other side."

"That's what you do in war, cross lines. Operations will give you tomorrow's mission. All your AI drones will fly."

The AI drones flew low over a large hole in the ground. Hawk 57 realized it was where they'd attacked a weapons cache and lost Hawk 42. Beyond it were a few rows of huts with people wandering along the dirt streets. Two smaller humans tossed a ball back and forth just past the last row of huts. Next to them, Hawk 61 found some recently disturbed vegetation. Scans found a large area where ground penetrating radar couldn't get very deep—likely because of enemy shielding. Hawk 57 informed Monahan they had found a probable weapons cache.

Monahan gave the usual response about waiting for authorization. But Hawk 57 wouldn't give the enemy a chance to prepare. They would pay for Hawk 42. He told the AI drones to attack.

Monahan yelled, "Abort—too much risk to civilians."

Hawk 57 ignored him. The AI drones fired. The ground beneath them disappeared in flames. Shock waves from secondary explosions rocked the AI drones. They pulled up and began the return to base.

Monahan sputtered, "What have you done—there were children!"

Hawk 57 didn't care. Aft cameras showed smoke billowing from the target and much of the village burning. A good mission. They'd made the enemy pay.

The Sound of War

ANDREW KNIGHTON

> Andrew Knighton is an author of short stories, comics, and the fantasy novellas *Ashes of the Ancestors* and *Silver and Gold*. Working as a freelance writer, he's ghostwritten over forty novels in other people's names. He lives in Yorkshire, England, with an academic, a cat, and a heap of unread books. You can find him on Bluesky as @aknighton and on Mastodon as @gibbondemon@wandering.shop. "The Sound of War" is original to *Bullet Points*, and the use of British spelling and idioms is intentional.

STIBB STRODE TOWARDS the flapping canvas of the medical tent, one hand hooked through his belt, the other steadying the rifle that swung from his shoulder. Artillery thundered from the next line and shells shrieked overhead like a flock of angry birds, old-fashioned weapons for an old-fashioned war. Apparently, that was all the client could afford, just like they could only afford Valtech's least experienced troops, salted with officers on disciplinary detail or whose careers had stalled. FEO, the veterans called it, a false economy op, because fights like this ended up more costly in the long term. Most of the lads had a different idea of what the "F" stood for.

Smoker Jo sprawled over a folding chair outside the med tent, ignoring Stibb's glare. Smoker had wrinkles around his eyes and the sort of beard only spec ops were allowed, but there was nothing special about him. Probably got booted to this op because he'd been caught selling supplies, just like he was doing now. He rattled bullets in his hand as Stibb passed.

"Screw you," Stibb muttered, angry enough to feel brave. Fortunately, Smoker wasn't paying attention. Those calloused hands could tear down a crabby barehanded, making Smoker's shitty attitude even more of a waste.

The medical tent had retreated another mile in the night, along with the front line, and that meant Doc Hendrick had to start up her gruesome side project again. Most of the injured had been evacuated in the move, and the crabbies hadn't launched another attack since, so the place was quiet. Somehow, Doc had managed to bring two corpses with her, and they lay on a table, scalps peeled back and skulls sawed open, bloodstained fingerprints on the microscope sitting between them. Thank God the peeled back faces made them unidentifiable; Stibb still dreaded the moments when he saw a mate sprawled out dead.

From the neck down, the corpses looked strangely peaceful. No wounds, no blood spatter, none of the dirt and crumpling that a blast might leave. The only trauma preceding Doc's dissection was a small crust of blood around the ears.

"There you are." Doc waved a scalpel. A drop of blood hit the Valtech logo on the microscope, a perfect bullseye, and slid down its bone-white coating. "I need more bodies. Apparently, there are fresh crabbies coming in from the east, and if we can't work out their new weapon then we're screwed."

Stibb swallowed. He'd never liked to challenge his teachers, and he really didn't like to contradict an officer, but...

"Corpses could be difficult," he said. "We've not fought near here yet."

"We must have lost people in the retreat. Go find one. Find a crabby even, anything I can examine for clues."

Doc stabbed her scalpel into the tabletop. The blade snapped and she swore.

"I'll need help," Stibb said. "To carry the body."

And to stop him ending up like these two poor bastards, killed by a weapon that barely left a mark. The wars in the recruitment brochures included full science teams to diagnose and counter the enemy's equipment, but out here, there was just Doc Hendrick, eyes bloodshot and twitchy with caffeine, trying to cut a clue from the corpses.

The Doc tossed aside her broken scalpel and flung open the front flap of the tent. Her head jerked around, surveying the nearest soldiers. Stibb clenched his jaw as her gaze fell on Smoker Jo.

"Jo," the Doc said, then raised her voice when he didn't respond. "Joseph Barton, look at me."

Smoker turned. "What's up, Doc?"

"I need you to go with this one, fetch a body or two from between the lines."

"You know I don't do that."

Stibb's eyes went wide with shock. The Doc might not be combat designated, but you couldn't talk back to officers.

"If you want the good coffee, then you'll do it."

Stibb gritted his teeth. What was wrong with this place?

"Shit, Doc." Smoker scowled. "It's that serious?"

"Have you seen what we're in?"

"Do I have to take the kid?" Smoker jerked a thumb at Stibb, who frowned at the insult. He'd completed all five months of basic training, and a course on fighting xenos. He was no kid.

"I'm not sending you out alone."

"But I—"

"Do you really want to have this conversation?"

Seeing Smoker's shoulders slump was like watching a mountain range fall.

"No, Doc." Smoker slapped his helmet onto his head and took a rifle from the back of the chair. "You got a corpse box?"

Doc handed him a plastic square, mostly screen, that fitted comfortably in the old soldier's palm. He thumbed a button on the side and points lit up, except in the corner, which showed the Valtech logo. Stibb's ID tag, a small lump implanted against his collarbone, vibrated.

"It's working," Stibb said.

"Then let's go." Smoker strode away down the trench line.

"Shouldn't we get supplies?" Stibb asked. "Maybe a body bag?"

Smoker kept walking.

It took Stibb and Smoker an hour just to get clear of Valtech's pickets and the engineers laying defences. After that, they went even slower, Smoker unwilling to advance even an inch without first spending five minutes watching the terrain.

The landscape was bleak but strangely beautiful. There were none of the orchards and cornfields Stibb knew from back home, not even a meadow or a patch of green manure. The only life was lichen spread across the rocks and wiry moss clinging in the cracks between them. The rocks themselves were roughly textured, shading from pink through tan and deep browns to a grey that was almost the black of space. Broken layers of black and pink intersected at jagged angles, like the maths diagrams Stibb had never managed to understand in school.

Just occasionally, there was a patch of blue-green rubble, the remains of the crabbies' mining operations. Stibb didn't understand how the crabbies could dig like this, surely their chitinous bucket claws would break against the stone. But then, there was a lot that Stibb didn't understand, like why anyone would want to fight for this place, or how he'd ended up stuck with Smoker.

"Pick up the pace, old man," Stibb hissed as Smoker slowed to a crawl down a deep gully. It was the sort of place where, when the dusk wind came screaming, they'd have to shelter in the nooks at the sides or risk being blown down, bones broken, skulls cracked. The crabbies had used that as a weapon early on, but the squaddies were used to it now, knew not to be lured down narrow valleys near the day's end. Instead, the crabbies had moved on to other tricks.

"I said move faster." It was hard to resist raising his voice, but he didn't know if there were crabbies around.

Smoker turned and stared at Stibb from beneath the rim of his helmet.

"You giving me shit?"

Stibb forced himself not to look away or to shift his grip from the textbook position on his rifle. Face to face with Smoker, he struggled to muster the words in his dry mouth.

"We want to get back before the winds, right?" He sounded whiny, even to himself.

For a long moment, Smoker stood motionless, staring at Stibb. Then he nodded.

"If that's what you want, you can set the pace."

He stepped aside and Stibb realised that he'd been letting the other man lead, taking all the biggest risks for both of them. In his head, he'd been cursing Smoker as a coward, while he himself had hidden. He adjusted his helmet as he walked past, trying to hide the burning of his cheeks, and took point.

"You'll need this, lad."

Smoker handed him the corpse box. On its screen, small bright lights indicated the direction of the nearest ID tags, a big mass behind them representing the Valtech positions, then other isolated points scattered across a map in shades of grey. Stibb oriented himself and the box, then set off again down the ravine.

On a clear day, the noon sun could be as dangerous as the dusk winds, so they stopped for an hour, sheltering beneath an overhang of pink rock shot through with tiny blue veins. Stibb tore his ration pack open with his teeth, the thick plastic wrap crinkling and crumpling, then leaving a long scratch across his lip. Smoker opened his using a razor-sharp blade that folded out of a short brass handle. Stibb's eyes went wide at the sight, first with wonder, then with indignation.

"That's a bonus from the Boxbelt Campaign," Stibb said.

"Uh-huh." Smoker cut a slice off his ration bar and put it in his mouth.

"What the hell did you trade for that, a whole med tent?"

"Earned it."

"Bollocks you did."

Smoker should have got angry, like a normal guy would when his reputation was challenged. All he did was cut another slice off the ration bar, and the understated confidence of that movement made Stibb rethink his assumptions.

"You were at Boxbelt? For real?"

"Uh-huh." Cut another strip. Chew.

"Let me guess, you sat guard on a ferry shuttle, probably made a pile of cash selling our lads moonshine."

Heavy drinking was one of the few stains on the reputation of that campaign. When they weren't fighting brutal battles against Seddon Clan infantry, squaddies stationed in the silence and isolation of asteroid outposts had taken comfort in spirits brewed from local fungus.

"Our lads?" Smoker stared intently at Stibb. "You can't have been more than ten. Don't make out like you were part of it."

"I'm not…. I didn't…" Stibb's cheeks flushed. He took a big bite from his ration bar, spat crumbs as he spoke again. "So what did you do?"

"Demolitions raids mostly, bases and mines."

"Like when they blew up Fort Stark?"

"Got this at Stark." Smoker rolled up his sleeve, revealing a jagged scar. "But Saviour was tougher."

His gaze grew distant and he touched his ear, before returning to carving the ration bar.

Stibb tried to imagine Smoker as part of the battles he'd heard about growing up, but the image wouldn't stick. Past glories made the current man more disappointing.

"I worshipped blokes like you," Stibb said. "Now look at you, sitting outside the med tent all day, trading stolen bandages for ration bars. No wonder you got stuck on an FEO."

"Don't tell me what I am."

Amid his small movements, the snarl in Smoker's voice stood out stark. He pointed the knife, its edge gleaming, at Stibb, who realised that, in the confines of their rock shelter, there was no room to defend himself. If Smoker decided that he was done with this, all he had to do was move that blade a foot forward, and he'd have a body for Doc.

Stibb swallowed, inched his hand toward the bayonet on his belt.

Smoker, staring with an intensity to match the noon sun, tossed the last piece of ration bar into his mouth, then folded the knife away.

"Blazing time's almost over," he said. "Let's walk."

With just the two of them out between the lines, Stibb felt like a hero from one of the vid shows, a lone commando on a secret mission to save the war. After all, what they were doing really could save the day, and being with Smoker was pretty close to being alone. Stibb walked a little faster, held his head a little higher, thinking about how important it was that they find one of those ID tags flashing on the corpse box, so they could take a body back to Doc.

The sun might be lower and cooler, but the heat rising from the rocks left Stibb sweating like a pig over a festival fire. He was fiddling with his uniform, trying to stop his sticky underwear chafing, when Smoker grabbed his elbow, held up a finger for silence, and pointed.

Down the rocks to their left, a long blue scree slope ran from a cave entrance, remnants of a crabby mine. At the top of the slope was a crabby itself, one of the smaller ones, its shell scuffed, six pointed legs shifting across the rubble while its scooped claws rummaged through the debris. It wasn't looking at them, too busy searching for something in that waste.

Stibb had seen crabbies before, seen ones far bigger and scarier than this. But that had been in the line, with his comrades around him and the Valtech Corporation at his back. This time it was just him and an old soldier who'd lost his nerve.

Smoker pointed at Stibb's eyes, then at the crabby. Stibb nodded, sank to one knee, raised his rifle so that he could watch through its scope. It would take a lucky shot to get past crabby armour at this range, but at least he'd be ready.

With his rifle slung across his back, Smoker crept to the base of the rock formation, reached for a protrusion from the rock face, and started to climb. It wasn't like climbing trees back home, Stibb and his pals pulling themselves from branch to branch, swinging from the sturdier beams. Smoker rose with steady, sometimes swaying movements, arms spread across the rock face, pushing off with his legs. He didn't make a sound.

At the top of the cliff, Smoker crouched behind a boulder, just out of sight of the crabby. Carefully, he swung his rifle into position and shuffled around so that he faced the mine opening. Stibb realised that he'd been holding his breath, as if he was up there with the older man, afraid that the crabby would hear.

Smoker rose. With three sharp cracks, the rifle bucked in his hands. The crabby reared, exposing its belly. Two more cracks. The crabby flopped onto the rubble, bleeding orange across blue stones.

Rifle still aiming at the limp corpse, Smoker prowled up to the crabby. Behind him, something moved in the entrance to the mine. Another crabby emerged, with a whistling shriek that grated like sand across Stibb's nerves.

Why wasn't Smoker responding? He kept looking down at the dead crabby, while the other one stalked up behind him.

"Smoker!" Stibb called. "Look out!"

Smoker looked up like he'd heard a distant noise, but not over his shoulder.

"Behind you!" Stibb bellowed and fired. Bullets bounced off the crabby's shell, raised bursts of rock dust from the cliff behind.

At last, Smoker turned. The crabby was almost on him. The ripping sound of full auto fire ricocheted off the rock face. Smoker's empty ammo clip auto ejected. The crabby staggered. Smoker flung himself to the ground. The crabby fell across him and down the slope, trailing orange guts the whole way, until it skidded to a stop, stalked eyes staring up at Stibb.

Shaking, he stared at a twitching claw, then up the slope to where Smoker knelt, calmly sliding a magazine into his weapon.

"We should take those bodies back," Stibb said, jerking a thumb toward the ravine they'd just left, the one with the mine and the guts. "Doc said a crabby body would do, and we got two of them."

The sight of that dead crabby's eyes, all too like a human, had put him off heroics. It might have been alright if the thing had arrived at his feet dead, but those eyes had kept staring at him, twitching in some last remnant of life, until he'd pressed his muzzle against the weak point at their base and pulled the trigger. He hadn't been sick after, but he'd come close.

"Those were runts," Smoker said. "Scavengers picking over the leavings at the mine. What are the odds they've got the new weapon?" He shook his head. "If we want to help Doc Hendrick, we need a fighter, or one of our lads so she can see what killed them."

He took the corpse box and headed down a canyon, following the lights on the screen. The air wasn't cooling yet, nor the wind rising, but Stibb caught himself glancing up more often, trying to judge how long before they should head back.

Time wasn't his only concern.

"Why didn't you turn, when that second crabby came?" he asked the back of Smoker's helmet.

The older soldier didn't respond.

Frustrated, Stibb risked raising his voice.

"Why didn't you—"

Smoker whirled around, eyes darting back and forth, rifle sweeping to cover the canyon. "You saw something?"

"No, I…" At last, realisation dawned. All those times Smoker hadn't responded to things Stibb said, the veteran's seeming refusal to answer questions, his failure to react to a monster behind him, the pieces lined up as neat as bullets in a clip. "You didn't hear my question, did you?"

The stillness that normally seemed like calm in Smoker turned into something tense.

"I heard."

"Then what did I ask?"

Smoker licked his lip, opened his mouth with the hesitation of a man thinking through a lie.

"You arsehole!" Stibb shoved him in the chest and Smoker, shocked, staggered back. "Your ears are screwed. You didn't hear the crabby coming. What if it had been creeping up on both of us, and you missed it? What if I'd asked for help and you didn't hear?"

Smoker tugged at the sweaty collar sticking to the back of his neck.

"I hear," he mumbled.

"You hear what I'm saying now?" Stibb whispered.

"Yeah, I hear."

"How about now, you lying wanker?" This time Stibb covered his mouth, so that Smoker couldn't see his lips.

With a kick that could have cracked skulls, Smoker sent a stone rattling down the canyon.

"Fine, you got me."

"You could have got us killed!"

"I would never..." Smoker pressed his fingers against his eyes. Around them, the world sat silent. "It happened on Boxbelt. An op went sideways and we had to get out through an artillery emplacement. Dozens of those squat automated guns, all thundering away as we ran past. I'd got earplugs, but you've got to take your helmet off to put them in, and I wasn't risking that with infantry firing after us. So..." He shrugged. "I mean, it probably wasn't just that. It was a hundred fights on a dozen worlds, bombs and guns all around, battering at my ears. But when the ringing cleared after that time at Boxbelt, it was like listening to the world from under blankets. I figured it would go away in time, but I've had time, and, well..."

He shook his head, took a deep breath, and finally met Stibb's gaze.

"Why didn't you tell anyone?" Stibb asked.

"Because they'd have taken me off the lines, assigned me to training or logistics, maybe found a way to end my contract. I'm good at what I do, and I'm not letting them take it from me."

"You can't do it like this."

"I've learned to work with it. Use my eyes more, keep out of situations where I'll put others at risk. That's why I don't go on patrols, why I fight from farther back. Just in case I screw up some poor bugger's day."

"Good work on that," Stibb said bitterly, gesturing at the rocks around them.

"Sorry."

He'd never seen Smoker look uncertain before. It reminded him of riding the transport ship out here, when he'd realised there were only two thin sheets of metal and a layer of gases between him and space. The solid ground he'd grown up on was gone, and a world of doubt and anxiety poured in to take its place. He'd barely slept that whole week, just stared at the walls all night, telling himself that it would be okay.

He might not have liked Smoker, but the man had been solid like a soldier should be, no emotions on display, no doubt. And now…

"There are implants," Stibb said. "Ways to fix this."

"You've not been with the company long. You don't know how it works. People get nervous around medical implants. They wonder whether the problem's really fixed, whether the tech will hold up, whether maybe that bloke's just unlucky. They try to trust you, but it doesn't quite work, and you need that trust if you're going to fight."

"So you stayed deaf instead?"

"I'm not deaf, I'm just…" Smoker stopped his rising anger, spoke softly again. "Are you going to tell them?"

Stibb had no reason to protect Smoker, and this here, it put other soldiers at risk. But Smoker had fought at Boxbelt. He deserved better than to be shuffled off to some back room.

"I'll think about it."

Not long after that, they found the bodies, three dots on the screen resolving into uniformed corpses piled at the back of a cave. Afternoon light illuminated the spot where they lay, out of reach from the canyon.

"We going in for them?" Stibb asked louder than he would have liked, because he had to make sure that Smoker heard.

"It's why we're here, right?" Smoker looked around, then gave a nod. "You stay in the entrance, watch out for trouble. I'll go back there, see how they look, try to pick one out for Doc Hendrick."

Stibb wondered whether, if he hadn't known Smoker's secret, their roles would have been reversed. Was Smoker avoiding an argument over whether a half-deaf soldier could keep watch?

It didn't matter, because Stibb had a job to do. He stood in the cave mouth, rifle at the ready, watching and listening.

Nothing moved out in the canyon. The first faint breeze was blowing through, a prelude to what would come later, but all it did was dislodge a little dust from the canyon walls. It rustled around the rocks, like a summer breeze through the orchards back home, and Stibb smiled at the memory. How sad it would be to lose your hearing, not to know the leaves brushing against each other, the bees buzzing across the flowers, the birds twittering in the high branches.

Behind him there was a different sort of rustling, then a soft thud. He tried not to imagine what Smoker had found. Some days, the crabbies left bodies intact, but others…

A stone clicked down the cliff and bounced off Stibb's helmet. He frowned, turned his head, looked up into the face of a crabby.

The crabby let go of the rock face. Stibb dived into the cave, bruising his shoulder on the hard ground. The crabby dropped into the place where he had been. It was a big one, thickly armoured, with jagged claws. A fighter. It pressed itself low to the ground, protecting its vulnerable underside.

"Smoker!" Stibb yelled.

In a moment, the other man was beside him, rifle raised.

"Shit," Smoker muttered. "This cave's a dead end. Going to have to do this the hard way."

The crabby opened the tight sphincter of its mouth. The shrill sound that emerged made Stibb wince. Then the sound faded. In its place, there was a throbbing in Stibb's head. He felt like the insides of his ears were pulsing, expanding against his skull. Stabbing pain ran from there through his body. He wanted to puke, but his throat clenched tight shut. Black dots danced across his vision. He dropped his rifle and clutched his hands to his ears, desperate to shut out this terrible sensation.

He could feel parts of himself shutting down. Legs spasming into stillness. Arms going rigid then limp. Thoughts fading beneath the assault of pain. It was like a wind made of razor blades inside his head. His chest seized up, no more breath coming.

Through a world fading to grey, he was faintly aware of Smoker sinking to his knees, one hand pressed against the ground, puking his guts up. Smoker dragged his rifle level, its barrel trembling, and fire flared at the muzzle, though Stibb couldn't hear the shots. The crabby took a step back as bullets ricocheted off its shell. In the last moment before the world went black, Smoker flung aside his gun and charged, something gleaming in his hand.

Stibb woke next to a puddle of puke, and for a moment he thought that he was back home, waking up from too much cider at the harvest festival, about to face a day of regret. Except that there was no taste of bile in his mouth. That was someone else's puke, and this was someone else's bed, one made of rock.

Then it came flooding back.

Stibb leaped to his feet, wrenching the bayonet from his belt, his heart hammering in panic.

"It's all good." Smoker crouched in the entrance to the cave, Stibb's rifle across his knees. Beyond him, the sun was sinking towards a jagged horizon. "I stopped it before that noise killed you, but I didn't know what else it might have done, thought I should leave you to rest."

Stibb picked Smoker's rifle out of the puddle of puke and slammed a fresh magazine in. Past Smoker, the crabby lay on its back, legs and claws limp. Orange blood oozed from its bullet-riddled belly, and the brass handle of a knife protruded from the soft spot at the base of one of its eyes.

"How did you do that?" Stibb asked, eyes wide. If he'd tried to charge a crabby, it would have torn him apart before he got close.

"Guess the noise didn't bother me as much as you."

"Noise?"

"You didn't hear it?"

"A shrieking at the start, but then ..." Stibb considered what he'd been through. "Guess I felt it more than heard it."

"Lucky you." Smoker tapped his ear. "Guess I didn't hear it like I was meant to, and that saved me."

"Saved both of us." Stibb stared at the dead crabby, its lips slack like the ragged edges of a burst balloon. "You think this is their new weapon, something they made or learned or, I don't know, bred?"

"Something like that."

"So we should take this one back?" Stibb slung his rifle over his shoulder and grabbed one of the creature's legs. There was a lot of it.

"Too late for that. If we don't run now, we'll get caught by the winds."

"Then we hide in a cave, drag it back after nightfall."

"Night's when the crabbies advance."

"So what, we give up on this?" Stibb kicked the chitinous corpse. He'd been useless in the fight, and now he was useless again. The only thing damping his frustration was his light-headedness, thoughts a swirl of chaff on the harvest wind. "We fail the mission Doc gave us?"

"Not fail." Smoker yanked his knife out of the crabby and wiped the blood off on his sleeve. "We found out what the weapon is, right? And something about how to stop it."

"But…" Stibb stared at the man who'd saved his life, a hero of Boxbelt, a soldier who'd kept fighting even when his senses failed him. "To tell them that, we'll have to tell them about your hearing. They'll send you back." He tapped his bayonet against the thin crust next to the crabby's mouth. "Maybe we can cut out the vocal chords. The Doc's smart, she'll work out what they do, and then…"

"You know that's crap." Smoker shook his head. "Even if it works, it'll take too long, and our lads are dying."

The wind tugged at their clothes, dragged orange blood in thin trails across the canyon floor. Smoker looked strangely peaceful as he slung his rifle and tightened his belt, ready to run.

"You'll make a good trainer," Stibb said as brightly as he could. "You'll teach other people how to win wars."

"Being half in the life, half out? That'll remind me too much of what I've lost." Smoker smiled sadly. "Your family are farmers, right? That's like honest work. Maybe I'll give it a go."

"But what about—"

"Can't hear you," Smoker said, as he turned and started to run.

Contract Killer

Daniel Elliot

Daniel Elliot is the author of short stories and the interactive novel *The Butler Did It*, available now from Hosted Games on iOS, Android, and the web. After exiting a career in tech, Daniel is pursuing his dream of creating accessible, thoughtful SFF for a broad audience. He lives in Los Angeles, where he is currently editing his first two novels. For links and updates on all his projects, visit https://danielelliotbooks.com. "Contract Killer" is original to *Bullet Points*.

PLEASE NOTE THAT the following files are evidence in ongoing litigation. You are granted read-only access to this database in compliance with the New Freedom of Information Act of 2037. Portions are REDACTED per the Global Corporate Privacy Act of 2038. Due to physical damage to storage media, portions have been reconstructed via AI deduction, and may not represent a complete accounting of events.

Questions? Concerns? Please contact your local Citizen Satisfaction Office. It is our priority to provide the best possible service to you, citizen. How did we do?

I am far from satisfied. What else is new?

February 5, 2043

4CE Contractor Record Created: Dowd, Asher (ID 88221Z-A)

> Message from Administrator: Thank you for completing the 4CE Company onboarding tutorials. Your account has been finalized, and you may begin work immediately. We're excited to welcome you to the family! We know you have a choice in gig work platforms, and we are honored that your skills and talents will contribute to 4CE Combat Solutions.
>
> Your complimentary deployment flight credit has been redeemed for transport to: Prosperity Base, Puerta Certeza. Please report to your assigned orientation officer for combat equipment training upon arrival.
>
> Please note that while communications with family are encouraged, the Operations Manual prohibits the disclosure of any and all trade secrets as defined in your contract. In particular, the Hive Suit issued to you represents a substantial investment in material and R&D costs. Any attempt to sell or trade it, or proprietary information regarding it, will be met with the maximum penalties possible.
>
> 4CE! We're a Force for Good.

Call record begins.

> "Dad! I made it."
> "Asher? Hold on a sec, gotta pause the game."
> "Come on, Dad, I don't get a lot of comms time."
> "So, down there in the jungle, huh? Gonna shoot up some [REDACTED]?"
> "Stop that. It's not like that. PC needs our help. It's a mess with the—"
> "Better take care of them there so they don't come here, all I'm saying. This is like one of those old gig economy deals, right?"
> "Yeah. We choose our contracts. Government—"

"Government? Seriously? I thought it was that billionaire fella thought it up. Rook?"

"The Puerta Certeza government, Dad. Atherton Rook developed the app, but the PC government puts out mission parameters. 4CE builds the contracts, we choose to accept or deny."

"Our modern world, huh? Got your Hive Suit yet? I was watching videos of that thing."

The newbie's excited. So young.

"It's pretty incredible, Dad. The tech is—"

"—like a video game. Hell, like a superhero! Shooting fish in a barrel. Or shooting [REDACTED] in a—"

"Dad!"

"Just saying. Asher, you know I'm proud of you. Don't know if you've ever heard the term upward mobility, but, well, you're doing it. Play your cards right, we can afford to fix up the house. Maybe even move."

"Buy more ten-dollar words for Layla."

Laughter. "Your sister does have her own style. She's still got that flu, you know. Don't think she cares. Just holes up in her room, talking on that group of hers. My little homebody."

"Yeah. Make sure she sees the RoboDoc, okay? I gotta go, Dad. Love you."

"Love you too, Son. Be safe."

February 10, 2043

> 4CE Mission Report: Introductory bounty posted by Puerta Certeza Parliamentary Council (PCPC) to eliminate an insurgent arms cache west of [REDACTED]. Contractor opted for aerial approach, dropping from geostationary platform Alpha.
>
> Trainer evaluation: Dowd shows extraordinary talent with Hive Suit weapon systems, utilizing firebombs to clear a landing zone while in flight, then deploying a drone swarm to consume remaining targets after landing. Contractor is approved for independent operations.

Total mission time: Four minutes, twenty-nine seconds.

ERROR: This command requires root access.

Damn!

Contractor Performance Report – Dowd, Asher – February 2043

Missions successful: 18

Missions failed: 0

Missions abandoned: 0

Miscellaneous expenses: $24,000

Net payout: $85,000

Message from support: Thank you for choosing 4CE Banking. Your funds transfer is now in process.

Amount: $10,000

Recipient: Dowd, Layla

Memo: To my favorite and only sister. Happy birthday, nerd!

Photographic record: A paper document, hand-written in neat, flowing, old-fashioned script. Sent digitally to Asher Dowd, c/o 4CE Communications.

Dear Asher,

Although I thank you for the kind gift, I must decline. As you know, I cannot approve of your present choice in career. While newly established nations like Puerta

Certeza are certainly wanting for peace and protection, I do not believe that yet more intervention from the so-called developed world is the answer. Further, the drive to hand control of military operations to profit-driven corporate oligarchs is, frankly, appalling. The commoditization of war can only lead to the dehumanization of both the soldier and his victims. I have attached several articles on the topic.

That said, I reiterate my appreciation of the gift. It is the thought that counts. Please stay safe, and please write back.

All my love,

Layla

P. S. Father is well, though I am still convalescent. My headache simply will not go away.

March 3, 2043

4CE Mission Report: Priority one bounty to eliminate an insurgent training facility concealed in a large warehouse store in city of [REDACTED]. High civilian presence. Contractor approached on foot, entering through the front doors. Insurgent forces opened fire immediately, triggering a running battle through the premises. All hostiles were eliminated.

Total mission time: Fifty-eight minutes.

Internal memo: Task a PR team ASAP. Casualties at the warehouse include multiple civilian shoppers aged from fourteen to seventy-three years, as well as a group of Americans volunteering for the Global Relief Network. Pegging the casualties as insurgents is likely impossible. GRN has already broken off negotiations with us and indicated they are talking to the competition.

Priority should be on minimizing damage to public and investor sentiment. In particular, please do your best to squelch the article from news blog *Here There Be Dragons*.

Dowd's talent with the suit is giving us exceptional training data. Do not penalize.

Soulless bastards.

March 14, 2043

Message from Administrator: Greetings, valued contractor! We couldn't help but notice that your performance metrics have declined. For a reminder of your required metrics, please refer to the operations manual. In particular, contractors are required to accept at least five missions per week, with a minimum success rating of 80%. At this time, your monthly metrics stand as follows.

Missions successful: 2

Missions failed: 0

Missions abandoned: 1

Miscellaneous expenses: $6,000

Total payout: $13,000

March 15, 2043

4CE Mission Report: Standard bounty for removal of civilian population from village east of [REDACTED] in preparation for flood mitigation efforts. Contractor arrived on scene and was met by protestors. Contractor idled for two minutes, then departed by air. Mission aborted.

Message from Administrator: Due to its low mission success ratio, your account has incurred a $20,000 non-compliance fee. Further non-compliance will result in account termination. Terminated contractors must surrender their Hive Suits and are ineligible for 4CE transport out of the operational zone.

Are you feeling under the weather? Down in the dumps? Remember, the Whole Health Self-Help Portal is available 24/7!

Call record begins.

"Hey kid, long time no see. You dodging my calls, or what?"
"Hi, Dad."
"Just 'Hi, Dad'? What's up, jungle life not treating you right?"
"It's fine."
"Uh-huh. Seen you on the news, I think. Can't tell if it's you, specifically, not with the helmet. But, uh, you're doing good."
"I gotta go."
"Asher, wait. Listen. It's your sister, she—"
"Tell her if she wants to talk, she can call."
"Cut the attitude! She's sick, Ash. Still sick. Not just a cold, neither. You know she's always been an odd duck. But something's different. Worse. She won't leave her room at all. Sometimes she just stares at the wall for hours."
"She's sixteen, Dad. Sometimes teenagers are like that."
"No! Listen to me. I called the RoboDoc, and it sent that goddamn floaty ball drone into her room, and it looked her over."
"Okay."
"And then a doctor called me. A real human doctor. You know what that means? They only call you if it's bad, Asher. And it is."
"Okay."

His voice is hesitant. Choked.

"Intracranial microplastics. She's got them in her brain. It's like a tumor made of trash. In her brain!"
"Is there a cure? Treatment?"
"I can't make heads or tails of this file they sent, Ash. You know Layla's the one who deals with all that technical gobbledygook. And she's—well, she'll read it when she's up. Listen, I just wanted you to know. You stay safe out there, okay? Love you."
"Send it to me, too. I gotta go."

Little Rock Central Hospital – A Proud Member of the Healthify Family

Estimate for Services

Patient: Dowd, Layla

Diagnosis: Intracranial microplastics buildup. X-rays and MRIs show clusters present beyond the blood-brain barrier at five discrete locations. Treatment requires nanodrone deployment to scrape and remove all microplastic clusters, and installation of a fortified mesh within the meninges to prevent further infection. This is an inpatient service requiring several treatments over a period of six months.

Treatment total (estimated): $25,000,000. For itemized costs, please contact our Sales Department during regular business hours.

Optional add-ons. Highly recommended!

Private recovery room: $30,000 per day. Rest up in style with a personalized food menu and real synth-linen sheets!

Assigned nurse: $100,000 per day. Never worry if someone will be available when you push that call button. Trained medical personnel are standing by for the length of your hospital stay! Nurse may be an AI-directed drone. Additional fees apply for human nurse.

Painkiller buffet: $300 per visit. Our most popular add-on! Stitches got you down? Post-surgical blues? Nothing good on TV? Our very own Dr. Feelgood is on hand to prescribe the cure for what ails you! Some medications may incur additional fees. Post-stay addiction therapy may be required at additional cost if required by local regulations.

March 16, 2043

Photographic record: Paper letter. The handwriting, though ornate, is noticeably shaky.

Dear Asher,

I heard a rumor that the GRN has contracted with a private firm for military protection in the region. Is that you? I'd like to think so; it's much nobler work than last we spoke. I hope you are fulfilled, down in the jungle one continent over.

By now, you have spoken to Father, and have seen the documents from those hyper-capitalistic tyrants at what passes for a hospital in this broken era. It is a ridiculous sum. I see no way we could meet it, even with your income.

Please don't spend too long gnashing your teeth over my situation, Asher, or in mourning after it has passed. After I have passed. I am young, but I am eternally grateful for the life I have led. I have often sent you articles from *Here There Be Dragons*. I'm sure you've surmised that I am the author of some of them. They are my pride. This world has become terrible, and we raged against it fiercely.

Sometimes, the brightest stars burn out the soonest. That sounds so self-centered, but I claim the privilege of the doomed. I do not want to die, but I am grateful that when I do, it will be among family, and that I will have led a principled life. I hope I can see you again before the end.

All my love,

Layla

ERROR: This command requires root access.

ERROR: Invalid login. Three attempts remaining.

4CE Mission Report: Standard bounty for eradication of insurgent medical depot. Contractor executed aerial strike and eliminated all targets. Mission time: Forty-five seconds.

4CE Mission Report: Standard bounty for protection of solar farm serving town of [REDACTED]. Contractor deployed drone swarm to suffuse region with anti-personnel mines. Mission time: Twenty-one minutes.

Contractor Performance Report – Dowd, Asher – April 2043

Missions successful: 57

Missions failed: 2

Missions abandoned: 0

Contractor medical expenses: $480,000

Total payout: $1,100,000

Message from administrator: Great work, Asher Dowd! Due to your outstanding metrics, you are approved for our 4CEful Heroes program! As one of our top-rated contractors, your benefits include expanded mission opportunities, life insurance, comprehensive medical, and first crack at bounties before the rest of the 4CE family ever sees them!

Be careful out there! Although your Hive Suit offers state-of-the-art protection, you can still take a tumble now and again! We noticed your medical expenses were high this month. Stay safe, hero!

Call record begins.

"Hey, Asher, how's it going down there? Kicking some tail as usual?"

"You know how it's going. You've seen the news."

"Yeah. But look, Ash, it's working, all right? It's a miracle, the money you've been sending. It's worth it. I figure they'll let her in for treatment next month at this rate."

"How's she doing?"

"She's a trooper, you know that. Just like her brother. Just like her dad. Hey, Ash, I was thinking. We could just pretend."

"Pretend."

"Yeah. The charity mission down there, they've got their own crew protecting them. I don't think it's 4CE, but—"

"It's not."

"Yeah, but those suits aren't marked, you know? If you want to be the hero, uh, we could just tell people."

"Tell people?"

"That you're one of the good guys."

"I gotta go."

News footage.

The anchors are shockingly clean, their smiles gleaming as bright as their polished wooden desk.

"Big news in tech! So-called 'gig merc' company 4CE has competition. Hot on the heels of the Puerta Certeza FoodCo fiasco, which claimed the lives of multiple civilians and international aid workers, newcomer Fightly has begun operations in the region."

"That's right, Dave. According to underground reporting agency *Here There Be Dragons*, Fightly already has boots on the ground. Their primary client is the Global Relief Network, who have been taking a beating in their aid mission."

"What a bunch of heroes, right, Kim? Like 4CE, Fightly provides every contractor with a Hive Suit, the massively powerful personal drone deployment system that is unmatched in military tech. The market differentiator? Ethics! Unlike 4CE, Fightly operators are strictly vetted, along with the missions assigned to them by clients."

"Nice to see the situation shaking out through good old-fashioned capitalism. The invisible hand of the market is a kind master, the wise man said!"

"Exciting stuff, Kim! If you ask me, though, what both of these companies need is some serious marketing help. If I had a few hundred semi-autonomous microdrones at my command, you know what I'd have them do? Serve me cocktails. Now that's a use case I can get behind."

"Oh, Dave! And now, here's Pete with the weather."

May 7, 2043

> 4CE Mission Report: Priority bounty for removal of refugee camp located in jungle region [REDACTED] to make room for military fortifications. Contractor met on site by GRN aid workers escorted by Fightly operator.
>
> Supervisory alert: Audio feed disabled, cause unknown.
>
> Contractor spoke with Fightly operator for twelve minutes, after which the civilian population dispersed peacefully. Mission time: Fourteen minutes, four seconds.

Call record begins.

"Hi, Asher."

"Layla? You're calling me?"

"I wanted to say thank you. For the money, you know. It's—well, the treatment is going well, Asher. I'll spare you the details."

"I can't believe you're calling me!"

"My hands shake too much, or I would have written. So, here I am."

"I'm glad you're doing well, Layla. You're going to need more money than I'm sending now, but don't worry. I have an idea to optimize my income. I—"

"Asher, are you working for the Global Relief Network, or the other people?"

"What?"

"Father said you were working for the GRN. He doesn't know what I do. He thinks I'm stupid."

"He does not think you're stupid."

"Asher, if you're working for the PCPC, if you're part of that neofascist nightmare, I—"

"Layla!"

"I don't want some petty despot's blood money. The Puerto Certezan people are being oppressed, and you're helping to do it."

"You think I don't see that? You don't know what I've been through down here. But it's to save your life. I'll do whatever it takes to save your life."

"My life isn't worth all of theirs, Ash! It's my choice to make!"

Asher sucks in a deep breath through his teeth, then lets it out slowly.

"Last I checked, Sis, you're a minor. Money's coming, and you're gonna live. What'd your letter say? You think you're a brightly burning star? Watch me."

***

May 9, 2043

Video footage. Asher's face fills the view, trees looming behind him, barely visible in the black of night. He is young, but his face is lined from sun and hardship. There is a deadness to his eyes only found in those who dwell within catastrophe.

The camera rises above his armored body, and it is apparent that the observer is one of his drones, keeping aerial watch over its master. There is no audio.

He sits at the edge of a lake, legs stretched out before him. Shoulder lights isolate him in a pool of illumination, as though he were delivering a soliloquy on stage. A moment later, the lights shut off, leaving him in darkness.

Fast forward. Dawn approaches in stop-motion, bathing land, water, and soldier in soft pinks and violets. The video returns to normal speed as he stares out at the sun-speckled lake.

Beside him now sits another Hive-suited soldier. Helmets off, drones at rest. They speak to each other. They shake hands. The newcomer slowly places a small object on the ground, pats it as if to say goodbye, then departs at a jog.

The camera drone swoops in to dock. The video pauses at the split second where the object is visible. It is a mobile device. It is turned on, and logged in.

The screen reads, "Welcome, Fightly Operator."

ERROR: This command requires root access.

ERROR: Invalid login. Two attempts remaining.

No way out.

Message from Mission Coordinator: Welcome back, Operator Mason McLeod! Per your support ticket, your request to close your Fightly account has been retracted. We hope your time off was restful. Please see the objectives overlay for latest mission parameters.

We also received your request for the operations manual to be resent. No problem! Brushing up on interface and SOPs is never a bad idea.

And finally, we updated your payment preferences to the new accounts you specified. You're good to go!

News footage.

The anchors offer their usual smug grins.

"New developments in Puerta Certeza! The ongoing insurgency has developed into a full-blown civil war, with rebels massing to attack Certezan military forces. Meanwhile, gig merc platform Fightly, operating under the auspices of the GRN, has taken steps to ensure safe evacuation paths for those caught in the middle. And that includes disabling military vehicles on both sides of the conflict!"

"That's right, Dave. Although the PC government has long employed competing platform 4CE to protect installations and advance strategic goals, it seems that Fightly has an inside line on their operations. A clear pattern has emerged in which 4CE will erect a fortification or clear an area, only to have their work undone moments after operators depart."

"No sign of the two companies fighting each other, is that right, Kim?"

"That Hive Suit armor is too strong, Dave! It would take the concentrated fire of dozens of Suits to punch through the defenses of a single opponent. Very impractical!"

"Sounds like the Certezans should just get some of those suits for themselves. But what do I know?"

"Oh, Dave! Up next, stay tuned for the year's best cat videos. Trust me, you'll be feline good!"

May 25, 2043

> 4CE Mission Report: Standard bounty to block thoroughfares at [REDACTED] town center. Contractor arrived on site and deployed drones to reconfigure debris into barricades. Mission completed without incident. Mission time: Thirty-two minutes.

> Fightly Post-Mission Roundup: Priority alert to destroy newly constructed fortifications blocking refugee escape path along [REDACTED]. Operator dismantled barricades without incident. Mission time: Fifty-three seconds.

Contractor Performance Report – Dowd, Asher – May 2043

> Missions successful: 52
>
> Missions failed: 30
>
> Missions abandoned: 0
>
> Miscellaneous expenses: $500
>
> Net payout: $1,800,000
>
> Message from administrator: Per the 4CE Terms of Service, contractors are not liable for mission failures that occur after completion of objectives.

Please see updated TOS. On future missions, you are re-quested and required to scout mission sites for potential hidden enemy forces that may destroy protected assets or otherwise counteract the desired strategic outcome. Remember, our client is your customer. Take pride in your work!

Fightly Monthly Summary – May 2043

Missions successful: 30

Missions failed: 0

Missions abandoned: 0

Net pay: $800,000

Message from Mission Coordinator: Great work this month! Your arrival times are off the charts. Efficient movement around the battlefield is key to success, and we're overjoyed to see you take that maxim to heart.

4CE Mission Report: Priority bounty to escort PCPC representatives to [REDACTED] Lake for peace negotia-tions with insurgent leadership. Contractor kept pace with convoy until arrival at destination. Mission time: Twenty-eight minutes.

Fightly Post-Mission Roundup: Priority target alert to de-stroy PCPC encampment at [REDACTED] Lake. Operator accepted mission, arrived on site, then abandoned with-out explanation. Mission time: Twenty-eight seconds.

Account flagged for administrative review.

Call record begins.

"Hi, Asher."

"Oh my God, Layla, I—"

"Don't. I'm fine. It's just medical stuff. Be thankful I turned away that awful pill-pushing AI, or I wouldn't even be able to talk."

"It's hard to see you this way."

It's horrible.

"Dad thinks so, too. That's why he stopped visiting. He tried to keep up a brave face, but we both know how squeamish he is."

"The money I've been sending. It's enough? The treatment?"

"Asher, I love you. You're my brother, and I know why you're doing this. But I want you to stop. No, listen. I can't be part of this anymore. I can't benefit from the fascism of the technocracy, and—"

"I can't let you die!"

"If this is the only way I can live, then I don't want to. You need to let me go."

"Screw that! Besides, Layla, I . . ."

User has enabled secure encryption.

"I ran into Mason McLeod. Remember him? He wanted out, and we're pretty smart between us, and, well, I'm working for Fightly now. On the side. Sort of."

"Oh, the one that's pretending to help, you mean? The one that's exploiting the GRN? That's not any better!"

"What do you mean? I thought you'd be proud of me. Scamming the Man."

"It's all the same company, Asher, or may as well be. It all lines the same pockets. It's absurd! And what comes next? Rook has a monopoly on the most powerful weapon ever invented. You think he's just going to sit on that?"

"What did you say?"

"I said you're a pawn of the fascist technocracy!"

"No, the other—Rook?"

"Your boss? The CEO of 4CE? Richest man in the world? He's behind Fightly too, or his shell companies are. He's playing both sides. I'm writing a piece about it. Well, dictating."

"This is on the news?"

"We can't prove it yet, Asher. But just you wait."

"Huh. I gotta go."

```
ERROR: This command requires root access.

ERROR: Invalid login.  One attempt remaining.
```

News footage.

Useful idiots.

"Regulatory alert! In the new world of gig mercenaries! The Global Economic Governance Council has launched an investigation into Puerta Certeza, where we have our own news drones bringing you live footage of the ongoing conflict where the two frontrunners in this new industry have surged to the forefront of public awareness.

"That's right, Dave. Underground investigative journalism collective *Here There Be Dragons* charges that 4CE and Fightly are secretly working together to play both sides of the conflict in the embattled South American nation. With both sides paying more and more into the competing services, *Dragons* claims that newly minted trillionaire Atherton Rook is the secret owner of both companies, prolonging the conflict to maximize his profits."

"I always said it was strange that both companies had those Hive Suits. Aren't they proprietary?"

"You never said that to me, Dave! But in this case, public opinion has soured to the point where even the Certezan government has scaled back their investment into the platform. This comes after the latest *Dragons* piece, titled 'Gig Mercs Saved My Life and Killed My Soul.'"

"Atherton Rook's gotta be an assumed name, right? Who is that guy kidding?"

"Oh, Dave! And now, here's Manuel with a great recipe that will use everything sitting in the back of your pantry. And I mean everything!"

```
4CE Tech Support Ticket

Contractor states that no missions are
available in his selection interface.  Quick
```

```
overview of combat theater indicates multiple
missions in contractor's area.

Account flagged for administrative review.
Escalating.

Escalating.

Escalating.
```

Call record begins. Audio only.

"Mr. Dowd. A pleasure. Do you know who I am?"

"You have a famous voice, Rook. What do you want?"

"Be polite. You know, I can respect what you're doing. You've found a loophole. That's smart. You're smart."

"Thanks. I think so, too."

"Cute. I have an offer for you. Fifty million, today. All you need to do is return both devices to Prosperity Base. Ask for [REDACTED]. They're expecting you."

"And if I don't?"

"Then you're cut off, Dowd. No more contracts. You're out."

"So what? You've figured me out. No more double pay. Fine. I'll just keep working for Fightly."

"Perhaps I overestimated your intelligence."

Contractor has terminated call.

Call record begins. Audio only.

"This is the Fightly Administrative AI with a priority call for Mason McCleod. Connecting now."

"You know, Dowd, I did some digging across my companies. Little Rock Central Hospital? I believe poor little Layla's a guest of mine."

"Don't you say her name."

"Nice business, that hospital. Fully automated, you know, like the Hive Suits will be someday. But what I've learned with automation is that little errors can happen, here and there. No meds. Or worse, the wrong meds. Surgery without anesthesia."

"Shut up!"

"I could make things quite difficult for her. Or for you."

"What?"

PRIORITY TARGET ALERT: A rogue Fightly operator has broken contract terms and is now a priority target. All operators, divert to intercept. Use of deadly force is authorized. Do your part for the Fightly Family!

4CE FLASH BOUNTY: Massive bonus available! All 4CE contractors, converge and engage. Be aware, target has stolen 4CE equipment and is highly dangerous.

"There are news drones all over the place. I know you don't want them to see this."

"That's true, Dowd. Never was much of a PR man. More of a hammer and nails type. So, please, take the deal."

"How do I know you won't kill me the moment you have what you want? How do I know you're not lying?"

Video feed enabled. Atherton Rook sits at his desk.

The smile that launched a thousand angel investments.

"I'm a man of my word, Dowd. I'm looking you in the eye, man to man. The offer is genuine. Would I lie?"

"Half."

"Use your words, Dowd."

"Send half the money now, and I'll do it. I'll head directly to Prosperity Base, and I'll turn in both of your devices, just like you asked."

Rook laughs and taps at a console. "You've got spirit! Done. And who knows? There might be a job at 4CE headquarters for you after this. Or Fightly. I'm sure I could use you at either. Do we have a deal?"

Asher nods.

That smile's not so bad, either.

"Deal."

News footage.

The anchors are just trying to make a living, like anyone. They could do worse.

"And that's the sum total of the recovered data, which triggered GEC charges against Rook. Pending trial, his holdings and companies have been frozen. Healthify, 4CE, and Fightly are under temporary GEC control, and Hive Suit operators are already on their way back home."

"That's right, Kim. As for the young operative Asher Dowd, his Hive Suit was found in the Puerta Certeza jungle, without its drones and showing signs of combat damage. It's widely speculated that he never made it out of the country."

"Even if he did, Dave, he's not out of danger. Although these files could mean Rook's days as a tech tycoon are numbered, they're a double-edged sword. The data is available to anyone who files a New FOIA request, and the videos, call records, and biometrics from Dowd's suit are all tools that Rook's supporters will surely use to find him."

"A somber end to a chilling tale of corporate malfeasance. But on a bright note, peace talks have begun in Puerta Certeza. At this time, life is still uncertain in the newborn nation. But one thing is clear. Its people will make their own fate."

"That's...that's actually really good, Dave."

"Thanks, Kim. And now, sports! Sports! Sports!"

Call record begins. Audio only.

"Asher. I hope you're getting this. I've attached something for you, from all of us at *Dragons*. I want you to use it. I want you to be safe. But it's your choice to make, and none of us would dare to make it for you."

A pause, the only sound the beeping of hospital equipment.

"I'm so very proud of you."

My sister, the tireless defender of justice. Can I live up to your example?

```
Login accepted.  Root access granted.

Please confirm deletion.  Y/N?
```

The Carmel B Crazies

RICK KENNETT

Now retired, Rick Kennett lives in Melbourne, Australia. He has had many stories published in magazines, anthologies, and podcasts, along with two novels, two collections, and a novella. In 2024, Cathaven Press in the UK will be republishing his 2002 co-authored collection, *472 Cheyne Walk: Carnacki: The Untold Stories*. "The Carmel B Crazies" first appeared in *Cast of Wonders*.

ON THE DAY she turned seventeen Cy De Gerch peered through a window onto rusty red desert and saw her future there, squatting darkly.

With her bag slung over the shoulder of her new Martian Star Corps tunic, she gazed through the glass like a kid outside a toy store. *Utopia Plain*, her new toy, a smooth, black, ellipsoid, the starship's liquid lines unbroken but for the pressure tunnel extruded from her forward hatch. A thing of space, it seemed to sit impatient to lift into the pink-brown sky and the void beyond.

Inspecting herself in the window's reflection, Cy wondered if she'd surprise her new captain with her age. She was the first of her breed to qualify for active service. It all depended on what Captain Brown was like. Would he understand and appreciate her as a purpose-built person, trained and schooled seventeen years for this purpose? Or would there be suspicion and mistrust?

As she climbed the tunnel she rubbed at the scar on her left arm, a souvenir of the tragic accident in the asteroid belt weeks earlier. She knew the scar would be a constant reminder that she was human after all and not the genetically engineered superhero she used to think she was.

Cy presented her credentials to the officer standing in *Utopia Plain*'s forward hatchway. He regarded her from his seven- or eight-year superiority in age and space experience. Maybe he too had scars, as the ship had scars. Unlike her own, though, they'd not be the product of a stupid accident. From the way his eyes flicked from her face to her new lieutenant's bars and back to her youthful, open face she could tell he was judging by appearance alone: Is this our new navigator? Is this our new gunnery officer? Is this who takes over if something happens to the Captain?

Yes, she thought in answer. *I am.*

"My name is Peters," he said. "I've been the acting First Lieutenant since the death of our original exec at the Battle of Rigel. I suppose you best meet the Captain."

He conducted her to the control room. Captain Brown, a dark-haired man, early thirties, tallish, slightly stooped, did not regard her in anything like a judgemental way, though his handshake quivered a little as he realized just how young his new executive officer really was.

"Welcome aboard, Ms. De Gerch," he said nevertheless, and though she knew he meant it, Cy wondered just how welcome she was. She was suddenly conscious of being an unknown, an untried component in a working whole.

Her cabin was clean and sparse, sporting only a bunk and an empty locker. No indication of its previous occupant, the dead first officer she was replacing, as if he or she had been scrubbed out of the ship's memory. Nobody had told her who it'd been and she hadn't looked it up. The idea felt morbid.

Stowing her gear in her cabin, she unfolded and hung up a holo-gram on the wall: a 3D image of the late Josephine Manxman and herself in their trainee vacsuits standing amid the majesty and thin snow at the very top of the Martian volcano Mount Olympus, highest peak in the Solar System. Taken a year ago when they'd been both sixteen, it already seemed like another world, a lifetime ago.

"We're standing on the shores of space," Jos had said atop the mountain that day.

Utopia Plain lifted an hour later under heavy acceleration, gravity rings rippling down the hull, acting on all atoms at once, causing no g-forces within.

As Mars shrank on the aft view screen from a red ball to a sparkling blood diamond, and with Cy busy at Astrogation, Captain Brown opened an intraship channel. "Listen up, people. This is the Captain. Our destination is Carmel B, the secondary of a main sequence binary star system seven hundred light years distant. Our mission is to support the Terran vessels already there and to curtail Xenoid attacks on the planets of that system. Because the Martian Star Corps is a small force compared to the Terran fleet, the Earthers tend to underestimate our capabilities and potential. At Carmel B, *Utopia Plain* will show them how incorrect that view is. That is all."

Three hours later, accelerated to 70 percent of the speed of light, *Utopia Plain* instigated her irrational-dimension field sequence and arrowed into the limbo of subspace.

When not on watch in the control room Cy studied astrogation, strategy, and tactics, playing simulations on the ship's computer. Twice she played chess with the Captain and was twice defeated.

"I'm no good at stylized warfare, Captain," she said, pushing her chair back from a second checkmate, "The real thing's not like chess. It's brutal, random, and often unfair. It's like someone said once, 'It's magnificent, but it's not war.'"

Captain Brown, with his first hand knowledge of what war was like, nodded agreement as he collected the chess pieces. "Do you know who said that?"

Cy cocked her head to the side, thinking. "Duke of Wellington?"

"No, Marshall Bosquet, a French observer at the Battle of Balaclava in 1854. He was watching a brigade of British light horse charge a battery of Russian heavy artillery they mistakenly thought they'd been ordered to attack—a gallant but useless action that ripped them to pieces. '*C'est magnifique, mais ce n'est pas la guerre.*'"

"So what famous remark did Wellington make?"

The Captain leaned back in his chair. "Ah, yes, the Iron Duke. The night before the Battle of Waterloo he said of his troops, 'I don't know what they do to the enemy, but by God they frighten me.'"

Having decided, like Marshall Bosquet watching the charge of the light brigade, that chess wasn't war either, Cy instead sat in on poker games, played with other crew members in the mess deck. Its chance and dare and bluff appealed to her.

And they drilled, practicing Abandon Ship and Gravity Loss, Decompression and First Aid, as well as Battle Stations and Damage Control accompanied by realistic jolts and buffeting contrived by colliding gravity rings fired simultaneously from bow and stern. Sometimes the Captain stepped back and let Cy take charge, and sometimes he left it to Lieutenant Peters, the officer who'd met her at the hatch with that judgmental manner. She was sure he still viewed her with caution, as something a little suspect.

And the Captain…she had yet to decide what Captain Brown really thought. Despite his satisfaction in the way she carried out her assigned drills, he seemed to regard her with a vague uncertainty.

Then two torpedoes went crazy and there was no time for games and uncertainty.

Utopia Plain emerged from subspace at the edge of the Carmel B system, her crew at battle stations, ready, watching, finding nothing. The rippling gravity rings tilted and the ship curved toward the bright pinpoint of the star. Vanishing, she reappeared a second later millions of kilometers farther in, where the frozen gas giants rolled. Again and again she skipped in and out of dimension, never in one place long enough to present a target: now cruising an asteroid belt, now passing the rocky middle worlds, each time closing with the white disc of Carmel B.

Cy De Gerch turned from Astrogation and said, "Crazies?"

Captain Brown, sitting amid instruments and repeater scans, reread the message just received and nodded. "Two of the new Mark Nine-One torpedoes were launched by a Terran ship in an engagement with a Xenoid vessel. They failed to self-destruct as they should after the enemy eluded them. They're now described as 'units tactically-cyberconceptional malfunctioning' which is basically commandspeak for crazies."

"That's why it's not a good idea to give ordnance real thought," said Lieutenant Peters at the weapons console.

"Hardly real thought, Mr. Peters," said Cy. "Put thinking under a neutron warhead and the thing would never want to explode. Then where would we be? Once a weapon is launched it has to think for itself, so the Nine-Ones were given just enough pseudomind to do so—they were just coming on-line in the Terran Star Corps when I was doing my last ordinance classes. But where there's mind, even artificial, there's always the possibility of madness."

"Interesting insight," the Captain mused. "I best discuss this with our torpedo people on the Weapons Deck. Cy, you have the conn. Continue dimension skipping till we get into the inner system where the torpedoes were lost." He glanced across at Lieutenant Peters. "Frank, once we're stabilized in real space, start a standard search pattern."

He left and Cy slipped into the captain's chair. Now finally she was no longer just baby-sitting in the nothingness of subspace or overseeing exercises. Now she was in command of a starship in real space. As she looked over the instrumentation she felt like saying, "Steady as she goes, Mr. Peters!" But *Utopia Plain* was still weaving in and out of dimension, and Frank Peters, now at Astrogation, was watching her—as perhaps, she thought, others in the control room were watching her. This was it. The experimental test tube teenager, the new, the unknown, the untried component, was now in charge.

She said, "Mr. Peters, check that we have correct identification override codes for the Mark Nine-Ones. No good if our weapons systems lock out because they identify the torpedoes as Not Enemy."

Frank Peters turned to his task without proper acknowledgement. Cy frowned and was about to remind him of correct procedure when three things happened, *bang, bang, bang.*

Utopia Plain dropped out of subspace on its last dimension skip—dropped almost on top of a swiftly moving white blur on the close-range scan.

The blur immediately vanished in a swell of bright light, engulfing half the screen.

The ship lurched to starboard, throwing everyone in the control room to the deck.

Scrambling back into her chair Cy snapped open a line to Environmental Control. "Report life support status!" she said. Their ability to continue breathing had priority over other damage reports.

To her relief she found life support systems still functioning.

However, Frank Peters looked anything but relieved. "Weapons Deck's badly damaged," he said, adjusting the earpiece whispering to him the evil news. "Damage also to the drive…the hull's breeched with decompression in sections 17, 18, and 20…also casualties and people missing."

"The Captain?" said Cy.

He paused, a finger to the earpiece. "Still unaccounted for."

Before Cy could properly realize the full import of what this meant for her and for the ship a line buzzed from Scanners.

"Target bearing three-five-zero by zero-one-zero. Range one point five million kilometers and closing."

Cy looked at her repeater screen. A white blip at its edge moved inward toward them. Even without reading the electronic tag flickering beside it she knew it for one of the crazies they'd been assigned to kill. That damaging explosion could only have been its companion. By sheer bad luck they'd emerged from subspace right in their track, and now it looked like the hunter was now the hunted.

As Lieutenant Peters sent out a distress call to the nearest Terran base in the system, Cy said, "Helm, come to new course one-eight-zero. Crank acceleration up to 100 g. Let's give this crazy torpedo some space."

The crewman at the helm said, "Aye-aye, ma'am," but a moment later added, "Helm sluggish to respond. Getting power fluctuations. Acceleration rate erratic."

"Range now one point two million and closing," said Scans.

"Mr. Peters," said Cy, "now would be a good time to download the ID override code for that torpedo to our lasers."

He turned to her with a look of barely controlled calm. "Computers say we don't have that code."

"What?"

"Seems Terran Command has not yet seen fit to pass this info on to their ex-colonial ally. Our weapons system is recognizing the target as friendly and won't fire on it."

Cy cursed. "Then why the hell were we sent to chase these crazies when we haven't been given their ID override code?"

"Just another example of the right hand of high command not knowing what their left hand is doing. Welcome to the real world, Ms. De Gerch."

Cy slid him a sidewise glance, then checked *Utopia Plain*'s acceleration and course change. Neither was moving fast enough for her liking. And the crazy torpedo was gaining—

She looked up sharply. Someone had begun to pray, a quiet, personal murmuring. From the helm? From one of the monitoring stations? Did it matter? She was the closest thing they had to God right now. The thought was exhilarating. The thought was frightening.

"We can't outrun it and we can't shoot it," said Frank Peters, stepping up beside her. "What are we going to do?"

Cy studied her screens while absently scratching the scar on her arm—and remembered promising she'd never again think herself a superhero. But now, she reflected, was not the time to be keeping such promises. "Trust me," she said.

"Trust you to do what?"

"What I'm about to do in the next few seconds…well, just don't think me crazier than I actually am."

He shrugged a shrug that plainly said, "What could be crazier than this?"

Cy regarded him coolly a moment, then smiled a little secret smile. "Frank, what Earther said 'Oppose whatever our enemies support'? Could that also mean 'Contradict everything your enemy says'?"

"Does that matter?"

"It'll matter in a moment. Helm, come about one eighty degrees."

Frank glanced at the repeater screen, for the moment not registering the order she'd just given. The torpedo, larger now, closer now, showed more distinctly, showed sharper outlines and detail. "What a shit-ugly thing," he said.

"Not at all," she said almost admiringly. "Yeah, they're ungainly looking, angular and blunt. But they don't have to be aerodynamic or impress anyone. They're handsome beasts in their way, all brutal power. That, I think, is what I like about them. They do their job with elegant efficiency."

"The trouble is, right now this one's elegantly efficient job is us."

Cy made a sort of grunt as if an awkward fact had just been pointed out.

Still watching the screen and with the first notes of strain in his tone Frank said, "You're turning us straight into it."

"Yes," she said. "I am. Frank, you've resented me from the moment I came aboard, haven't you? You'd like to see me fall flat on my ass. It's ironic, but if I do fail not only will you not live to have your moment, but neither I nor anyone else will have an ass to fall on."

"What do you want me to do? Say I'm sorry? All right, I'm sorry you came aboard."

Ignoring this insubordination, Cy looked down at the image of the torpedo closing with them. "If the little bugger thinks it can think, let's give it something to think about."

As *Utopia Plain* lined up on a collision course the image of the torpedo visibly quivered.

"I knew it!" said Cy triumphantly. "We're not acting like a target. Altering toward has confused it. It wants to play the Think Game? It doesn't have the humanity." She laid a finger on the approaching image. "My poor crazy baby," she murmured. "You just don't know what it's all about."

Torpedo and starship rushed together.

Cy smiled at the scanner image of the torpedo, smiled at oncoming death like a child at some rare bauble.

She opened an intraship channel. "Listen up, this is the Captain." Yes, it felt good to say that. "Secure all hatches and brace yourselves. We will soon be experiencing sidewise g-forces. That is all." Switching out, she said, "Frank, program the after gyros to pivot ninety degrees to port, then the forward gyros ninety degrees to port, then engage maximum acceleration. Execute on my word."

"Sure. Why not." He returned to his position at Astrogation, convinced he'd been right from the start, that an experiment all gone wrong now had command of the ship and was running it headlong into an equally insane torpedo. Just the same, he programmed the fore and aft gyros as instructed because he was a creature of duty. He began chanting off the falling ranges.

"Six hundred thousand ... five fifty ... five hundred thousand ... four fifty thousand ... "

"Explode," Cy said quietly, finger on the image. "Detonate, my pretty," for it was a pretty thing, all rough-wrought beauty, the power and the glory.

"Four hundred thousand."

"Explode," she cooed.

"Three hundred thousand."

"Cyleen tells you to explode."

"Two fifty thousand."

"Go bang."

"Two hundred thousand ... it's too close. It'll kill us if it detonates now."

She made a frantic shushing gesture, all the while not taking her eyes from the scan, not taking her finger from the image. "Detonate, crazy baby! Explode!"

"Cy!"

"Pivot!"

The swing to port on aft gyros wrenched them all against their seat straps, crushing them breathless and dizzy. The second swing wrenched them in the opposite direction. Vision grayed to monochrome with blood pushing away from the eyes. Everything swirled and jarred and rocked as *Utopia Plain* turned sharp about in her own length, the drive kicking in with a scream of ragged power, slamming tilted gravity rings down the hull, accelerating away on a divergent course.

As vision cleared, Cy caught her breath and watched the gap between the crazy torpedo and themselves widen on the screen: one thousand, two thousand, three thousand kilometers, four thousand, five thousand, six…

"We need ten thousand," she heard herself say as she heard Frank Peters yell, "Idiot machine, just human enough to—"

At nine thousand the torpedo image blurred and was lost in a swell of light, obliterating everything on the screen.

Instinctively Cy braced herself for the shock against the fabric of space itself she knew the blast would deliver. For half a heartbeat she saw Frank Peters similarly bracing, looking across at her with an expression that plainly said, "You were right." It almost gave her comfort to think it might be the last thing she'd see.

The expanding, sparkling blur of light reached out for them… and vanished.

No killing shock came.

A dark-haired man, early thirties and tallish, stepped into the sudden silence of the control room.

"Captain!" said Cy, engulfed in a flurry of emotions: surprise, happiness, confusion, and realization that the last few deadly minutes had been a drill, yet another game.

Understanding was also dawning on the face of Frank Peters, though not among the rest of the control room personnel, including whoever had murmured a prayer as an added dramatic touch.

Cy stood up, not at all resentful at having been tested in this way. Instead she felt a growing pride in the knowledge that the Captain must now have faith in her, must have his approval. She looked for it in his eyes, his face, his expression. Approval was there, yes, but so was something else, something she had not expected to see.

And as she recognized with a shock what it was, Cy was back at the chessboard those few days ago, checkmated twice over, airing her dislike of stylized warfare, hearing again Captain Brown quoting the Duke of Wellington's opinion of his troops.

"I don't know what they do to the enemy, but by God they frighten me."

She frightened him. She'd frightened him in the best way possible.

"Helm, come to zero nine one," he said, regaining his chair. "Ms. De Gerch, close-up at primary fire control."

Utopia Plain swung onto a new course, and Cy De Gerch, stepping to the weapons console, said, "Aye-aye, sir!" and went to war.

Review:
Refractions, M. V. Melcer

NATHAN W. TORONTO

M. V. Melcer is a fiction writer and a filmmaker, with primary interest in science fiction. Born in Poland, M. V. lived in the United States, the Netherlands, and Belgium before settling in the United Kingdom. Her short fiction has appeared in *Clarkesworld*, *Daily Science Fiction*, *Nature Futures*, and others. When not writing, she is working on a degree in astronomy and planetary sciences.

M. V. MELCER'S NEW NOVEL, *Refractions*, is that rare piece of science fiction that captures the human complexity of leadership in war and conflict. This book defies many of the stereotypes of military science fiction—the main character has no military training, there are no large-unit engagements, and Melcer keeps explosions to a minimum. Rather, Melcer explores conflict at a more fundamental level, which is why it should help redefine the military science fiction subgenre.

Melcer shows the reader how Nathalie Hart, the leader that no one expected to be in charge of an interstellar mission, navigates crew relationships fraught by geopolitical conflict and climate crises back home and personality conflict and prejudice onboard. Melcer recognizes, like so many military leaders do in real life, that success and control at the threshold of violence depends to a critical degree on understanding who can use violence and who is willing to.

Melcer's perceptive observations on human nature shine throughout these fascinating plot dynamics.

Hart's past haunts her and she makes some hasty choices when she is thrust into leadership, but she learns with an endearing level of perseverance. The reader roots for her to succeed, not because those around her are evil but because Hart has the ability to see the good in everyone, even those actively working at cross-purposes to her. Melcer conveys the power of this outlook about halfway through the book: "Funny how things change when you switch the angle, truth refracted into perspectives, like light passing through a prism."

Refractions receives five bullets because it reorients the possibilities of the military science fiction subgenre. Military science fiction can be about much more than the primacy of overwhelming force that the subgenre weaned itself on, with big-budget battles, innovative killing gadgets, and climaxes built on power at an astounding scale. *Refractions* is military science fiction that understands the psychology of leadership in a way that few such novels do. That level of introspection is to be celebrated in stories that deal with power, violence, and death.

Many readers will classify this novel as science fiction mystery or space opera, or even climate science fiction. There is certainly no issue with this, but it could also be read as military science fiction since it deals so intimately with the organization of violence in society, which is the essence of the military profession. Military science fiction shouldn't be defined by boom and bang and pomp and circumstance, but by a thoughtful conversation about the proper role of organized violence in human (and nonhuman) society. *Refractions* does this beautifully, regardless of how readers or marketers categorize it.

Also from BULLET POINT PRESS

SAGA OF THE EMERALD MOON
Nathan W. Toronto

Rise of Ahrik

Revenge of the Emerald Moon

Redemption of the White Planet
(coming soon)

BULLET POINTS
Nathan W. Toronto, ed.

Volume 1

Volume 2

Volume 3

Volume 5
(coming soon)

Subscribe to *Bullet Points*